TIME TRAP

By
ROG PHILLIPS

ARMCHAIR FICTION
PO Box 4369, Medford, Oregon 97504

*For more information about Armchair Books and products, visit our
website at…*

www.armchairfiction.com

Or email us at…

armchairfiction@yahoo.com

A DOORWAY INTO THE FUTURE...

When two well-known nuclear engineers crossed a common telephone with the latest kind of nuclear induction units, they got a lot more than they bargained for. In fact they got something that even Alexander Graham Bell could have never imagined in his wildest dreams—a telephone with a direct connection into the future! And there was a voice on the other end of that connection…a human voice. But just whom did this voice belong to and what did her whispered words of warning really mean?

The two astonished engineers, Joe Ashford and Ray Bradley, were soon knee-deep in the creation of a time machine that could carry them into the distant future, a future where the United States was threatened by a horrible three-eyed menace from Earth's past.

FOR A SECOND COMPLETE NOVEL, TURN TO PAGE 133

CAST OF CHARACTERS

RAY BRADLEY
A man of remarkable engineering skill and ingenuity, he created a working time machine from a plain old phone line.

NELVA
She was "the voice" at the other end of the line. What was her motive behind helping two men from the distant past?

JOE ASHFORD
He didn't think time travel was possible, or that a time machine could ever work. Now, here he was, stuck in the far-off future.

VAL NELSON
At first glance his interest in helping the newcomers appeared to be gallant and altruistic, but appearances can be deceiving.

ARTHUR GRANGER
Leader of a subversive organization called the "Custodians." But what were they guarding and for whom were they guarding it?

THE VARG THROTT
A human-like alien race, they appeared out of nowhere and quietly infiltrated—then took over—American society.

VARGIA
Queen of the Varg, her picture was everywhere, and so were her spies. Would the rebel forces get past her unremitting vigilance?

CHAPTER ONE

"HELLO?" It was a pleasant feminine voice, Ray Bradley winked at Joe Ashford, his business partner, and cleared his throat nervously.

"Pardon me for disturbing you," he said talking into the phone. "But—could you please tell me what the date today is and what time it is now?"

"Are you the same young man that called me up and asked me that two years ago?" came from the telephone receiver. Then, "Yes, I suppose you are, the voice is the same." She paused and then continued, "Well, all right. It's ten o'clock in the morning, June fourth, nineteen sixty-one. Now please don't disturb me for another couple of years."

"Thank you, ma'am," Ray said. "I won't, I promise." He dropped the receiver back on the cradle of the quite ordinary looking telephone that rested on the glass top of the quite ordinary office desk. The rather large case on top of the desk in back of the phone was far from ordinary in appearance, however. Its glowing tubes and strangely shaped wire coils were like none in a radio set. And the cord from the phone that led into this weird instrument, became lost in its bewildering maze, and reappeared again at the back of the case to connect into a standard telephone wall receptacle.

Ray leaned back in his chair and tapped his fingers on the desk in thought. To his right was a large window opening on the graveled roof of the next door building. At his back across the small office was a frosted glass door with lettering in reverse, spelling out "R. A. BRADLEY, J. G. ASHFORD, CON-SULTING RADIONICS ENGINEERS."

The pencil behind his ear went into his fingers and came to life, scrawling dates and figures on the note pad at his elbow. A moment later he took an electric etching pencil and wrote,

"7.026.16," and etched a short line at the edge of the dial so it would line up with the guide mark on the panel of the black box.

"There," he said, straightening up. "That's the mark for seven years, twenty-six days, and sixteen hours in the future. Now—"

He moved the dial with the vernier screw so that it advanced not quite a quarter of an inch of its perimeter into the uncalibrated part. Then he dialed the same number he had just been talking to.

"Hello?" The voice held the same, slightly questioning lift, the same pleasant welcome; but there was a barely noticeable change.

"Hello," Ray Bradley said. "Could you please tell me the date and the time again?"

"Oh. It's you," the voice said. "I've often wondered when and if you would call again—and the years have passed up to now without your doing so. Twenty of them, in fact. It's August fifteenth, nineteen eighty-one, two-thirty past-my-lunch, as my granddaughter says."

A pleasant laugh came from the phone. Ray took the opportunity to write down the date and time she had given.

"You know," she continued, "if you are a bashful suitor you'd better hurry up. I'm seventy-one years old now."

"It's one of the regrets of my life that I didn't look you up back in about 1950," Ray said, and really meant it. "Goodbye—and I love you for helping me with the dates."

He hung up quickly, a lump in his throat. Moments later, when he had etched the markings on the dial of the black box, he inspected the progression of those marks.

"Time passes faster on the dial settings as we go farther and farther into the future, Joe," he commented.

"From the amount of blank dial left," Joe said, "you can go maybe several hundred years into the future. But tell me how the thing works. I still don't get it."

Ray Bradley leaned back in his chair, crossed his legs, and lit a cigarette, his eyes resting fondly on the unornamented black box hooked into the phone wires between the phone itself and the wall connection.

"I don't understand too much about it myself," he confessed. "About six months ago I was monkeying around with a sort of Rube Goldberg circuit—a takeoff on the circuit for the nuclear induction setup developed in 1947 for identification of substances by their magnetic moments of induction. The meters I had in the circuit didn't behave right. They would register when they shouldn't, and not register when they should.

"It took me two months to figure out the amazing conclusion that they were registering electric impulses that were in the past or the future, instead of in the present. I studied my circuit and finally figured out that with my wire coils I had constructed a sort of unfolded four-dimensional magnetic field, and that by varying it ever so slightly I could pick up future or past currents in a wire and bring them into the present.

"From there it was only a short step to the setup in that black box. It works both ways. When I speak into the phone it sets up the normal fluctuating current. That current goes into the time field and sets up a similar fluctuating current in another time. Then, when that woman answered, the fluctuations in that future time worked back through the field to our present.

"It works something like a radio. With a radio you change the natural frequency of the circuit by changing the settings. Then that frequency builds itself up, while all others dampen themselves. With this setup I have in the black box I probably contact a fourth dimensional extension of the current in somewhat the same way. If I could only figure out some way to transport actual matter over that gap we would have time travel."

"Hey! I just thought of something," Joe said. "Call up our own number a short time in the future. Then you can talk to yourself."

"Hmm," Ray said, intrigued by the idea. "Maybe you've got something."

He carefully set the controls of the black box for twenty-four hours into the future and dialed his own number.

"That num-ber, has bee-enn dis-connected," a semi-mechanical recorded voice said.

"What?" Ray said. He listened to the voice repeat its message and then laid the phone back on its cradle slowly, a frown on his face. He looked at Joe, frowning. "This time tomorrow the phone's disconnected…"

"I had a hunch something like that would turn out to be the case," Joe Ashford said. "I'll bet if you rang this phone with the setting at yesterday you'd be out or something."

"Or something," Ray Bradley grinned. "Since I have no memory of receiving the call, naturally I'm not going to make it. Why tempt fate? Anyway, I'm more interested in calibrating the dial. I'm going to call up my telephone sweetheart again when she's eighty and see if she's still alive."

He dialed that number after setting the dial for an estimated fifty years into the future. It was a male voice that answered, deeply resonant, with a slight hint of foreign accent that was more an over-carefulness of pronunciation than an actual accent.

"I know this is going to sound a trifle silly," Ray said smoothly, winking over the phone at Joe. "But would you be kind enough to tell me what time it is and what the date and year is?"

"It's May third, nineteen ninety-nine," the voice said promptly. "The time is—oh, eleven fourteen. I don't think you're being silly. By the way" (the voice chuckled throatily), "what's the date and time where you are?"

"That's a good question," Ray said. "It's four in the afternoon, July seventh, nineteen fifty."

"And you expect me to believe that?" the voice asked banteringly—but Ray was not listening.

In his mind—it was definitely in his mind, a voice was talking to him. It was a woman's voice, filled with a note of urgency and insistence. Something about it stirred him strangely so that he was at first not quite conscious of what she was saying.

"Leave the place where you are at once. This very instant," she was saying. "Please! If you don't you will be destroyed, *leave!*"

Then the urgency in her voice gripped him. He dropped the phone without bothering to hang it on its cradle.

"Come on, Joe!" he ordered, jumping to his feet and running toward the door.

"What's the matter, Ray?" Joe asked, following, and catching up with Ray.

"I don't know," Ray said, taking the steps down to the street from their third floor office-laboratory two at a time.

As they burst into the street they were knocked off their feet. A split second later came a soft *whooming* breath, which rose upward and outward from the building they had just left. Debris hit the sidewalk and the street around them, missing them miraculously.

Cars were screeching to a stop. A man and a woman ran screaming into a doorway across the street seconds ahead of an avalanche of bricks.

In the space of a slow breath it was over. The quiet was vividly intense, then erupted into blowing horns, excitedly babbling voices and, in the distance, the growing sound of sirens.

Ray and Joe, still hunched on their hands and knees at the entrance of their building, looked at each other, white faced.

"There's why your phone is disconnected tomorrow," Joe said shakily.

"Yeah," Ray said, standing up. "Let's get out of here before we have to answer questions."

Three blocks away on a side street they plunked some nickels into a jukebox and settled down in a booth over cups of coffee.

"What I want to know," Joe said slowly, "is—how did you know it was going to happen?"

"I didn't, Joe," Ray said. "It was—well, this'll sound crazy; but a voice spoke in my mind—not over the phone. It was the voice of a girl. She told me to get out of there fast. The way she said it I couldn't help myself. I had to do it—and we made it out by split seconds."

"Telepathy, huh?" Joe kidded grimly. Ray nodded.

"And fifty years from the future," he added. "I'm sure of that. You know, there was something funny about the voice of that fellow I was talking with, I mean queer-funny, I don't know what. It reminded me of that recorded voice telling me my phone is disconnected, only I'm sure it wasn't a recording. There was something inhuman about it. That girl, though. Mmm. It did things to me."

"I'll say," Joe grunted. "When you ignore your coffee it's because you're in love."

"She's beautiful," Ray said dreamily, ignoring Joe's remark. "I know she must be. I wish there'd been time enough to find out more about her. That date was May third, nineteen ninety-nine. I want to remember that."

"I'll help you remember it," Joe said dryly. "The question now is, what do we do now? Rebuild your time gadget? Call up more numbers? You know, I wouldn't be surprised to see a couple of nice blondes walk in right now and say they had a date with us. That would be nice—to rebuild that thing and turn it back into the past and make dates for us right this minute."

"Ha ha," Ray said. "You think of the funniest things. Ha ha."

"It was only a passing thought," Joe shrugged. "The coffee's enough. And it's going to take all our extra dough to get another office and equip it, and rebuild your gadget."

CHAPTER TWO

RAY BRADLEY slept restlessly. It was a hot July night. He and Joe Ashford had looked at three different office spaces and half decided on one on the fringe of the factory district, then spent the time after their late dinner discussing plans for rebuilding the time circuit that had been destroyed by the mysterious explosion.

After going to bed Ray had lain there puzzling over that explosion, and how someone in the future could reach across the gap of time and accomplish it. The biggest question, however, was *why*. Why would anyone want to do that? To destroy that time bridge and the one who had invented it, of course—but why? There seemed no answer.

And so his thoughts had turned to the mysterious mental voice out of the future. It had bridged the gap of time without using that circuit. The mind was a mysterious thing, little understood. Undoubtedly its structure was able to be affected by cross currents in time as well as space in much the same manner as, the time circuit could alter or pick up variations in electric currents in the future—and certainly fifty years hence lots of things would be known about the mind and its powers that weren't known now.

A lonesomeness crept into Ray's thoughts. He tried to laugh it off. "Here I've never met the gal," he thought. "I don't know her name nor what she looks like—and I'm lonesome for her." But with that thought came the feeling that he would know instinctively it was her if he passed her on the street tomorrow.

And with thoughts of the girl of the future in his mind, a longing for her, a wistful yearning toward her, he finally fell into a deep sleep of exhaustion. Almost at once he heard her voice.

"This is Nelva," her voice formed in his mind. "I've been waiting for you to fall asleep. When you were awake you were too full of thoughts and anxieties for me to reach you."

"Nelva," Ray said in his mind. There was an intense satisfaction in his thoughts at the knowledge of her name. It was, he felt, a name that would fit her perfectly: strange, alluring, musical. The vision of a beautiful face formed with vague cloudiness before his mental eyes, and he didn't know whether it was her actual face, or merely something he imagined and constructed out of his inner desires.

"You must listen to me, man of nineteen fifty," Nelva said. "What is your name?"

"My name's Ray Bradley," Ray answered. "What caused that explosion that destroyed my equipment and most of the building?"

"There's no time to speak of that, Ray," Nelva said, and the sound of his name as she spoke it was a caress. "Tell me what you know of your time bridge in the telephone circuit. Do you understand how it works—or was it an accidental thing?"

"I understand a little, Nelva," Ray said. "Its secret lies in three coils placed mutually at right angles to one another—and a fourth that in some way sets up a four dimensional interlocking of magnetic fields so that a current in the wire generated at some future time alters a current existing in it in my own time."

"I see you understand enough, Ray," Nelva's voice formed. "As your thoughts focus on the knowledge I am able to read much more that is in your thoughts than you bring into consciousness. You must come here to my time. We—I need you."

"But how?" Ray asked. "That circuit is barely able to be affected by almost non-existent currents in your time. I certainly can't cross the interval between my time and yours with it."

"You can," Nelva said firmly. "Those coils are interlocked by magnetic fields—and magnetic fields can be made strong enough to do powerful work. Fastened into a machine to protect you from harm, more powerful coils can draw you out of your own time and send you forward into mine. It's quite safe. Only you must hurry."

"Hurry?" Ray echoed. "But why? If I can travel to the time I wish, I can take a year to build it—and land in your time right at the instant you are speaking to me right now."

"It isn't as simple as that," Nelva said. "But there's no time to explain. You will learn all those things later. And I can't talk to you any more right now, I'm risking everything each instant this conversation continues. Varg Thrott can trace my thoughts back to me from you."

"Who's Varg Thrott?" Ray asked. Suddenly he was wide-awake and sitting up in bed. There was a sense of a horror just barely missed—as though his forming of the name of that creature had conjured it into present existence—almost. Was Varg Thrott the name of the man he had been talking to over the phone? It couldn't have been. Varg Thrott wasn't the name of a man. Of that he was sure. It was perhaps the name of something alien—extra-terrestrial.

There was some terrible threat existing in nineteen ninety-nine, able to reach across the years and destroy in the past—*now.*

If Varg Thrott had a time travel machine he could even come back physically and hunt him down and kill him before he could build his own time machine.

Yes, there was danger; but it was danger that couldn't be avoided nor dealt with until it came. He and Joe would have to be forever on the watch for it, and work fast. It might even be a good idea to move away somewhere and not let anyone know where they were, in case there was an attempt to trace them through their old office...

He opened his eyes and was momentarily surprised that it was broad daylight. A word sounded in his thoughts. It was clear and bell-like, the sound of a church bell over a countryside; the crystal gracefulness of tone of a fountain of water arching into a deep pool. It was the name of the girl of the future. Nelva!

He spoke it aloud, flavoring its sound. Then he frowned, for another name came into consciousness, sinister as the dark clouds that presage a storm, Varg Thrott. Now, awake, the name sounded even more sinister and alien than when he had first heard it while asleep.

He leapt out of bed, feeling that only with action could he shrug off the growing feeling of danger. A cold shower sent tingling needles over his skin and left him refreshed and wide-awake. Pausing at the phone, he called Joe Ashford and told him to meet him at Tony's, their usual eating spot in half an hour; then he dressed.

Outside the sun was shining. The sky was a clear blue. People walking on the sidewalk were cheery and oblivious of the fact that time had been bridged, the future opened to one man of the year nineteen fifty.

He was five minutes ahead of time, but Joe was already there. Ray slid into the booth and gave his breakfast order to the waitress. Then, swiftly, he told Joe what had taken place during sleep.

"Nelva?" Joe exclaimed. "Hmm. Nice name. Why didn't you ask her if she had a friend? I'll bet you didn't even tell her your old sidekick Joe would be going with you."

"I don't think you'd better go with me, Joe," Ray said. "In case anything happens to me there should be somebody here that can do something about it. I'll build another telephone gadget so I can reach you by phone."

"That's what you think," Joe said. "But you'd better think some more. I'm not going to be left out of things while you have all the fun. Who knows? I might even look up my great grandchildren while we're in nineteen ninety-nine and spend a week or two with them and find out who I married?"

"Great grandchildren?" Ray echoed. "Fifty years isn't that far ahead. Why, we might even find ourselves still alive... How would you like to drop in on yourself?"

"That's an idea," Joe grinned. "I could talk over old times together."

"You know," Ray persisted, "it's possible. We'd only be seventy-five fifty years from now. Lots of people live that long."

"Not unless they get something to eat," Joe said as the waitress laid their food on the table.

"And not unless they keep from getting knocked off," Ray added after she departed. "We've got to drop out of sight while we build the time machine. Varg Thrott might come looking for us. Nelva, I feel sure, can find me anywhere."

"Or any time," Joe said dryly. "Imagine being married to a dame you can't hide from."

"Who would want to?" Ray shot back.

"And how do you know this character out of a nightmare, Varg Thrott, can't do the same?" Joe asked. "Maybe after running around finding a hole to climb into we'd find it was a nice booby trap he or it had coaxed us into with our own fears?"

"We'll have to chance that," Ray said. "It can't be any more dangerous than sitting on the fence where he can see us or track us down."

"You're right," Joe agreed. "And we'd better get busy on it right after breakfast. Got any ideas where we should hole up?"

"A long ways from here," Ray said. "For two reasons. One, then we won't have to be afraid to go out on the street. Two, I imagine the time machine will remain stationary in space while going forward in time, and we should get to nineteen ninety-nine well away from this neighborhood, because this neighborhood will be watched, probably all along the time line from now to then."

"That's right," Joe said. "When we get there we don't want to set down in a nice little circle of Varg Throtts and stand helpless while little Nell is tied to the log that will be run through the—hey!"

He dodged the slice of toast Ray threw at him and laughed uproariously. Then they both sobered and ate in silence, their eyes almost unconsciously studying everyone that entered the cafe.

After breakfast they stopped at the bank while Ray borrowed several thousand dollars and signed papers permitting the bank to collect directly the royalties due him from three of his paying inventions. With the money in small bills they caught a taxi and followed the maneuvers anyone picks up in detective stories to shake pursuit. They saw no one that looked suspicious, but, as Ray said, "Better to play it safe."

Finally, sure that no one could have followed them, they rented a room on the opposite side of town. Two days later they were at work in a small shop room they had rented.

Joe, drawing on the skill at heavy construction he had gained in shipyards and a small factory, devoted himself to the task of building a sturdy steel chamber that would hold back anything except a titanic outside force.

Ray concentrated on the design and the building of the drive coils and the self-contained power source. The big unknown was how long, in their conscious time, it would take for them to reach the year nineteen ninety-nine.

At the end of the sixth week the time machine was finished. Nothing in the shape of a threat had materialized. And, though Ray often mentally called Nelva, there wasn't the faintest whisper of answering thought. It was as if it were all fancied and unreal. Only the time machine kept them from slowly growing to feel it had been a dream.

Ray had installed automatic controls, not knowing whether time travel would make them unconscious or too ill to stop their forward flight into time or not.

"We'll set the shutoff relay for one minute from now, ship time," he said as they stood inside the machine ready for departure. "That may be a day or a million years. We'll have to find out the hard way. If we're still alive when the relay shuts off the coil setup, one of us can go out and find out what day it is. That way we can gauge our time jumps better."

16

He and Joe looked gravely at each other, then his hand pushed in the switch that sent current through the coils. Instantly they felt a searing pain shoot through them that seemed to drag at every cell in their bodies. It seemed that it would never end. Abruptly it was gone as the coils cut out at the end of the minute.

"Boy," Joe exclaimed. "I don't want to go through *that* again."

"Let's go out and see if we traveled any into the future," Ray said. "While we're at it we might be able to get something to ease the pain."

Joe twisted the wheel that drew in the locking bars on the hatch cover and pushed it open. The dust on the floor outside was thick and without footprints. "We went some, anyway," Joe commented. "I wonder if we just disappear, or seem from out here to be here all the time?"

"What difference does it make?" Ray asked.

"None," Joe said. "Except that we only paid our rent on this place for three months. They might blow us up to get us out unless we keep our rent paid."

"Problems," Ray groaned. "Why didn't I think of that? Well, let's go out and find out what date it is before we think of anything else."

Out on the street things seemed no different than they had last seen them—except that the building they had just left had the appearance of being deserted. Its windows were opaquely grimy.

At the first corner they came to was a coin operated newspaper vending machine that had not been there before. Ray found his fingers trembling with a mixture of feelings as he fished in his pocket for a nickel and shoved it in the slot. There was a *whirr* of inner machinery as a paper came into view in the chute at the bottom.

With Joe at his shoulder, he opened the paper and looked at the top for the date. It was May 19, 1957. Instantly Ray's thoughts were working on the calculations to convert a minute of time travel to the time traveled. This was quickly shattered by a deep groan and the sound of Joe falling to the sidewalk.

He turned, took in Joe's sprawling form, and crouched, his eyes exploring the deserted street for some sign of attack. There had been no shot.

Still watching warily, he sank to his knees to see whether Joe was still alive. His fingers found a wrist and felt for a pulse. It was there, slower than normal, and weak. Risking surprise, he concentrated on Joe and made sure there were no wounds. Then, stuffing the newspaper in his hip pocket, he lifted Joe and ran back to the building and laid him on the floor in the time machine.

Taking only time to bolt the building door, he entered the time machine and closed the hatch cover. Now, safe from almost any form of attack, he concentrated on Joe.

Joe Ashford's face was deathly pale, his breath barely perceptible. Whatever had struck him down, Ray concluded, had been noiseless and hadn't left a wound. Therefore it must be some diabolical weapon of Varg Thrott.

He felt for the pulse once more. It was still slow and weak; but even as he felt it, it quickened suddenly and grew stronger. Seconds later Joe's eyes fluttered open. He lay there, his face expressionless, a dazed look in his eyes, Ray waited. Suddenly—

"Let me look at that paper again," Joe said in a completely normal voice.

Ray eagerly complied, almost ripping out his pocket to get the paper out quickly. Joe took it and read the date aloud.

"Are you all right?" Ray asked anxiously. Joe looked up at him blankly.

"Sure I'm all right," he said. "I fainted."

"Fainted?" Ray asked, unbelieving.

"Yes," Joe confessed matter-of-factly. "All the time I didn't really believe we could do it. Somewhere in the back of my mind I always believed this was a lot of hokum. It wasn't until—well, until I saw the date on that newspaper that I fully realized we had actually traveled in time—or outside of time—

to the future. It just struck me that's all, I was like a poker player that's been having a lot of fun believing it's for fun and then suddenly discovers the chips he's been playing with are for big money. I fainted." He looked at the ludicrous expression on Ray's face. "What's the matter? You look like you'd been cheated—oh! I see what you were thinking. You were thinking that Varg Thrott had—"

He doubled up in a fit of laughter. "Oh," he groaned. "This is rich. I'll bet you carried me all the way from the corner with the feeling that Varg Thrott's fiery nostrils were panting down your neck!"

"Shut up," Ray growled. Then he joined in the laughter. Finally they sobered a bit. "It just goes to show, though," he said. "All this time we've been afraid of this unknown threat that can reach down from the future and has power enough to blow up a building. When you fainted the only thing I could think of was…It's struck!"

He picked up the newspaper and looked at the date once more.

"We've got to figure how far we go," he said thoughtfully. "We don't want to overshoot 1999. We traveled six years and ten months, approximately, in sixty seconds of time travel. Is that constant? Or was it something like dipping an oar into a stream to shove a boat along—in other words, did we hook back into the normal time flow instantly, or drift a bit like a floating boat?"

"If it's constant," Joe said, "then a little more than six more minutes of time travel will get us there—I mean get us 'when.'"

Ray tossed the newspaper in a corner and set the automatic adjustments of the controls.

"I'm setting it for three minutes," he said. "Think we can put up with the pain for that long?"

"Hey, wait a minute," Joe exclaimed. "I just happened to think. There's a bottle of aspirin in my bench."

He was back quickly. He and Ray each took three, washing them down from the thermos of coffee in their food cabinet. They waited several minutes, then Ray started the machine.

CHAPTER THREE

THE NEWSPAPER carried the date, May 19, 1999. The newspaper itself was different than those of earlier years. It was put together like a magazine, pocket size, with slick paper that seemed to be some sort of plastic rather than a wood fiber pulp paper.

There was something peculiar about arriving at that date. The time machine had stopped three different times at that date. Each time Ray had gone back a ways in time and tried again to land in May third. Finally Joe had gotten an idea and silently worked it out.

"Look, Ray," he had said. "Six weeks ago in our lives you were talking to someone in May third, 1999. We seem to be able to land only in May nineteenth—or several years before 1999. Maybe there are only certain moving points in time that you can insert us into with your time machine."

"That must be it," Ray agreed sourly. "That would tie in with Nelva's insistence that we hurry—when it seemed there was no need because we could land at any date. She must have known that every minute we wasted was wasted beyond recall."

Ray and Joe stood by the news vending machine and glanced through the paper curiously anxious to find out something about things. Joe chuckled suddenly.

"I just thought of something," he explained. "We're like a couple of guys in a new city looking through the paper to see what the local news is like—and we've never left town—still inside the city limits."

"That's right," Ray agreed, surprised. "I hadn't thought of it that way, but subconsciously my mind had substituted distance for time. I guess the mind has a habit of trying to make things seem normal and according to past patterns to itself, like your not believing we were actually traveling in time, until you saw the date in the newspaper." He grinned at Joe.

"Rub it in," Joe said. "But—the more I think of it the more I realize I wouldn't have come if I'd really believed we could get here. And speaking of being here, what do we do now? Too bad you don't know Nelva's address."

"Now that we're here," Ray said, looking at the street and buildings around him, "I find it hard to believe that this Varg Thrott business is real. Everything looks too—"

"Too prosaic," Joe said. "I'll bet we pass a policeman before we go three blocks, and I'll bet he'll nod to us if we look at him, and walk on. I'll bet we can go into a cafe and get a cup of coffee and hand them a 1948 quarter without somebody saying, 'Oh, looky! Two boys from 1950! How unusual…'" He put one hand on a hip and went into an act as he said this.

"Yes," Ray said reluctantly. "I'm beginning to have a sinking feeling that Nelva and Varg Thrott are figments of a dream. Still, if that's so, what caused the explosion? And how account for Nelva's voice in my mind, warning me?"

"Maybe she's your guardian angel," Joe suggested hopefully. "Anyway, let's look around and see the sights. We can give the town the once over and then run back to our own time in time for supper."

Ray kicked at the sidewalk that seemed to be made of something like concrete and plastic mixed together.

"Did you notice?" he asked. "All the buildings in this neighborhood—the buildings that were here in 1950, are torn down and new ones in their place—except the one where the time machine is? And, though we only paid three months rent, no one else seems to have ever used it. I wonder why?"

"Is it important?" Joe asked. "Me, I think it's a lucky thing for us. What if we had come to a stop right in the middle of something built since 1950. We might have found concrete floors and steel girders running through us."

"I don't think so," Ray said slowly. "Just the same, I've got an idea. Let's decide to stay here a couple of weeks or so. Then let's send the time machine back to our own time with the controls set so it will return in two weeks."

"Can we do that?" Joe asked in surprise. "It might be a wise thing to do. Otherwise someone might find it and use it. Then we'd have to build another to go back home in."

"It'll only take eight minutes to get back," Ray commented as he locked the hatch cover from the outside. "Let's stand over near the door and watch what happens when it starts. Maybe we'll find the answer to why this building has been left alone."

He and Joe stood by the door of the building. Ray watched the second hand on his wristwatch as the seconds ticked by.

Suddenly the time machine seemed to blur. Then it was gone. But now they could see why the building had been left alone. The opposite wall loomed close, as though seen through an invisible magnifying glass. And the entire building had tilted. That opposite wall, instead of being across the expanse of a level floor, seemed at the foot of a steep incline.

Ray turned his head and saw that the wall and the door at his back seemed to lean precariously over them. Joe looked too.

"Let's get out of here," he said hurriedly.

Outside, the building seemed normal. They studied it in wonder, then stepped back inside. Instantly the wall was leaning over them again.

"You go out and I'll stay here," Ray suggested.

Joe stepped outside. Instantly, to Ray's eyes, he seemed to become a foot taller. He saw the expression on Joe's face.

"Hey! You look shorter," Joe exclaimed.

"That explains a lot of things," Ray said, stepping through the doorway onto the sidewalk beside Joe. "Imagine anyone even trying to tear the building down with all the space distortion in there. No wonder it was left alone."

"But how can the wall lean inside and not outside?" Joe asked.

"It doesn't," Ray said. "We lean backwards when we're inside, and don't realize it. That's what makes the floor seem to tip downward, too. There's a force that draws us toward the place where the time machine was, and we lean back to compensate for it. Since we think we're standing up straight, we judge everything by that."

"That's like that mystery spot down in Santa Cruz that we went through once," Joe said. "Do you suppose that could be produced by a time machine going through?"

"Maybe," Ray said. "That field must be a kind of wake in space produced by the passage of the time machine as it passes, and since it passes every instant, that wake would exist in every instant, even though the time machine has already gone into the past or the future."

"Wait a minute," Joe said. "Our ship didn't go into the future yet. It went into the past."

"I know," Ray said. "But don't forget, it has also passed this instant going into the future for our date with it two weeks from now."

"We should have brought the aspirin with us," Joe groaned. "I'm getting a headache from all this time travel business."

"Our time machine is out of reach," Ray said. "Let's find a drug store. They'll have a phone book. We can hunt up the address of that phone number. After that we can go look the place over. We'll have to start from there—unless I hear from Nelva via telepathy."

"Yeah," Joe murmured elaborately. "Wonder why she hasn't called you?"

They began walking, lapsing into silence as their eyes explored the changes in things around them. The streets were paved with something that looked and felt like the blacktop, so widely used in 1950; but it was as springy as foam rubber, and there were closely spaced small holes in it that gave it a waffle-like appearance.

There were no power or telephone poles anywhere. On the corner across the street from the newspaper vending machine was an oblong cover flush with the sidewalk that had the words, "FIRE DEPT.," molded into its surface.

So far they had seen no one; but now a man turned the corner ahead of them and came toward them. They studied him with concealed eagerness. He would be the first human being they had seen since leaving the year 1950.

He was disappointingly ordinary. His suit, showing signs of wear, but neatly pressed, was almost the same cut as their own. He passed them without looking directly at them, and went on without looking back at them.

"It looks like we'll at least blend into things," Ray said with relief. "I was a trifle worried that styles would have changed so much we would stand out like sore thumbs. But—I wish now we'd stopped that man and asked him a few questions. We might even have been able to find out who or what Varg Thrott is. Oh well." He shrugged his shoulders.

At the corner they decided to go the way the man had come. Two blocks away could be seen the lights of neon signs. People were plentiful ahead. It was a business corner.

They passed more people, all ordinary in appearance, and all of whom passed them without more than casual glances. There were show windows lining the sidewalk now. The things displayed were recognizable, and might have been "next years model" of many things existing in 1950. There was only one major difference in shop windows.

Where, in 1950, there were statuesque mannequins, unmoving signs, and neatly lettered prices, here in 1999 the clothes dummies went through repeated motions such as one, a lifelike golfer, going through the motions of striking a ball—and actually hitting one that was instantly replaced by another as the tee dropped beneath the floor and rose reloaded. The individual letters in all signs also went through continual gyrations. Everything moved—hypnotically, compelling the attention of passersby.

In the window of a sewing machine store there was a dummy housewife, running a dress through a sewing machine. Her hands made the expert manipulations necessary to keep the material in line. At first it seemed the dummy must be a live person—until close inspection showed that no thread was being sewn into the cloth, and that the dress was going round and round over and under the sewing machine table.

Forgotten amid all these wonders of advertising developed into a fine art were the reasons for their being here, and the threat of the mysterious and now unreal Varg Thrott. They gazed enraptured as country people visiting a city for the first time.

At last they came to a window in which a gentleman dummy filled a glass of water from a real faucet, dropped an Alka Seltzer like tablet into it, held it until the tablet dissolved, and then actually drank it—every thirty seconds. Gyrating in the background, yet somehow preserving their order of spelling, were letters announcing that *Sooth-a-Seltz* dissolved eight-tenths of a second faster than any other brand.

"Ah! A drug store," Joe said. "You know, with all this movement of stuff in store windows I'm beginning to feel seasick, Ray."

"Then take a *Sooth-a-Seltz*," Ray said, grinning. "I'm beginning to like all this."

"Like it?" Joe said, pulling up short in the doorway of the store. "I think it's ghastly—a horrible monstrosity created by fifty years of hundreds of shrewd schemers thinking up more and more ways to make you advertising conscious."

He shuddered realistically and pushed into the store. Ray Bradley followed him. Inside, it looked much like an ordinary drugstore of the modern 1950 type. There was a string of phone booths at the far end. They started toward it, walking down the aisle next to the lunch counter.

They were directly in front of the picture on the wall behind the lunch counter before they noticed it. They stopped abruptly and looked up at it—frozen.

It appeared to be a twice as large as life, three dimensional photograph in color of the type that portrait photographers all over the country were beginning to feature in 1950.

It was the head and naked shoulders of a seductively beautiful girl; but one thing after another leaped from that picture into shocked awareness. Her pointed chin and smooth curve of jaw were dainty and elfin. Her skin was creamy perfection in texture. Her hair was a billowing dream of rich golden clouds. But—her forehead was high, and wider than it should be, and in its center slept a dreamy eye of milky blue, resting above two slanting lines of eyebrows. Beneath those lines, as on another face almost, were two eyes awake, normal in size where that other was enormously large; and one of them twinkled with merriment and laughter from blue-green depths, while the other stared with cold gray frigidity and inhuman cruelty—arrogant.

The face—each of the two awake eyes seemed to sound the spirit of each side of that superhumanly beautiful blend of feature. The red lips brought into juxtaposition two spirits, one smiling and innocent, resting lightly on the upturn of the lips under the mischievously twinkling eye, the other cruel and sadistic in the slight downward quirk. The whole was monstrously beautiful.

In vivid crimson above the head, seemingly far in the distance and large, were letters of melting strokes saying, VARG THROTT.

"God," Ray heard himself mutter. He became aware that people around him were looking at him and Joe uneasily. The normal conversational noises were suddenly hushed. The silence seemed to hold fear—and menace. He felt his eyes drawn back to the picture on the wall. By an effort of will he forced himself away and dragged Joe with him, on toward the phone booths.

"Snap out of it, Joe," he muttered. "People are beginning to notice us." Inside he felt a growing, icy numbness. There was no possible question of doubt—that three-eyed head was that of Varg Thrott—and Varg Thrott was a woman, and not human.

He glanced back across the store and saw the dozens of eyes upon him, fear and suspicion lurking in their depths. Across the store at the entrance people were crowding out, whispering to those who were coming in, who then turned and joined those leaving.

"Cripes," he heard Joe grumble at his back. "How can I find the address of that number? You have to know the name."

At the front of the store the tide of escape was suddenly reversed. People were stumbling and falling as they were pushed back by uniformed men—men a foot taller than those they were pushing, and in whose foreheads rested that third, tumor-like eye of milky blue.

Ray felt a tug at his coat. He turned. A hand was motioning for him to follow from the depths of the phone booth. He didn't hesitate or question. He jerked Joe out of his concentration on the phone book. The arm in the booth vanished. The back wall of the booth was an open door.

"Come on, Joe," he whispered; and stepped through. Joe followed. The secret door closed and heavy bars dropped over it. They were in a narrow passage between walls.

"That was awfully close," the man who had rescued them said grimly. "The Vargian police will probably tear the store down to find this passage now. What was the matter with you two? Don't you know better than to act suspiciously in the front of a Vargian spy screen? There's certain to be a monitor watching." He pulled his lower lip angrily. "Lucky you had sense enough to guess your only escape would be back by the phone booths, though. Otherwise you'd be on your way to the local torture center and blabbing your guts out."

Joe opened his mouth to say something, caught the slight warning shake of Ray's head, and remained silent. The man who had rescued them turned and led the way along the narrow passage to a dead end—which slid aside when he touched his toe to a spot in it. They passed through and made a right angle turn into another passage between walls, so narrow they were forced to turn sidewise.

At the end of this second passage they climbed down the rungs of a metal ladder to the basement level. Their rescuer lowered the cover back into place and bolted it, then, without a backward glance, crossed to the wall of the basement and touched a spot that opened part of the concrete wall into a brick lined tunnel.

The tunnel was short, opening into a round concrete bore barely five feet in diameter that stretched ahead into darkness.

CHAPTER FOUR

HALF AN HOUR LATER their rescuer led Ray Bradley and Joe Ashford into a bricked side passage that ended against another of the secret concrete doors that formed a part of a basement wall.

There were no lights. They kept together by holding hands until they reached the foot of some steps leading upward.

"Act casual," their rescuer warned. "And—my name's Val Nelson. This is the hotel I live in. I'll make out like you were just in for a short chat, and you can leave openly without any trouble or questions."

"Hotel?" Ray asked. "Then how about our getting a room here? We don't have a place to stay yet."

"Oh?" Val Nelson said, coming to a stop halfway up the stairs toward the crack of light underneath a door at the top. "Then that explains your carelessness. I've heard that the Varg Thrott pays little attention to things that go on in the country. For the last couple of weeks the police have been acting like they were on edge about something. The slightest suspicious act brings down a dozen or so of them with questions and clubs and even mass arrests."

"Nobody knows why?" Ray asked, reaching out in the dark and squeezing Joe's arm in a warning.

"No," Val said. "Let's go up. I'll go out first and make sure the hallway is clear. Maybe the room clerk'll have a couple of vacant rooms for you. What's your names?"

Ray told him. They continued up the stairs. Ten minutes later they were safe in a large room overlooking the street from the third floor.

"You're safe for now," Val said. "If you don't mind, I'd like to bring a couple of friends over to meet you. They're probably around the hotel somewhere, so I won't be long."

"Sure," Ray said. "Go ahead."

"Why didn't you tell him where we came from?" Joe asked as soon as Val Nelson had gone.

"Just playing it safe," Ray said. "We don't know who he is—or anything else about the setup here. It's better to keep our mouths shut and our ears open until we find out more. Anyway, do you think he would believe us? It doesn't look like my discovery of time travel took. I wonder why?"

"*My gosh yes,*" Joe muttered. "We built the time travel machine in 1950. If we patented it or turned it over to the government or anything, it would almost certainly be well known by now, and he would have come to the conclusion we are from the past by himself."

"It worries me," Ray said. "We could be killed and never get back to our own time, you know. That would be the most logical explanation for the world of 1999 not knowing about time travel."

"But the Vargian police know about us," Joe said. "Did you get the connection? He said they had been on edge for the past six weeks. That would be starting with the date that you made the telephone call."

"Yes, I got it," Ray said. "That means that there's a general alarm out for us. What do you make of those police and the picture of that girl? That third eye—*ugh*. It gives me the creeps."

"They look like something out of a fantasy book," Joe said. "I wonder? Do you suppose they could be some race from another planet that landed and took things over with their superior weapons? An invasion from Mars sort of a thing?"

"That could be," Ray agreed. "Or maybe they're a mutation of the human race brought on by the atom bomb. That third eye—the one of the girl in the spy screen—it didn't seem like it could focus with the other two. Maybe it isn't an eye even though it looks a little like one. Maybe it's some distinctly new sense organ."

"Like maybe telepathy?" Joe suggested. "Able to contact a mind fifty years in the past?" He looked at Ray queerly.

"You mean Nelva might be like that picture?" Ray asked, his eyes holding horror. "That would be awful. Or maybe it wouldn't. I don't know, I don't know what to think."

He turned abruptly and went to the window. Joe looked at his back with pity in his eyes.

There was a brief knock at the door. Joe opened it, Val Nelson and two others stood there. He opened the door wider and invited them into the room.

Val solemnly introduced the two newcomers. They were Craig Blanning and Neal Smith, both quiet, broad-shouldered, around twenty-five the same as Joe and Ray. Val was older, perhaps in his forties.

Neal Smith came right to the point as soon as introductions were over.

"Val told us all he knew about you two," he said. "How about telling us more? Where are you from? How did you know about the secret entrance to that drugstore? I want to warn you that you're in a spot. It looks to me like a setup. In other words, you two could be a plant. Val shouldn't have brought you here. He should have turned you loose after letting you out in some alley."

"What'll happen if you don't believe the story we give you?" Ray asked.

The two newcomers looked at each other with humorless smiles. Val Nelson looked uncomfortable.

"So it's that way," Ray said. "Well, let's get it over with then, because you wouldn't believe us if we told the truth, and I doubt if we know enough about things here to get by with a lie."

"If you don't talk," Craig Blanning said, "we'll just have to find ways to make you. How about letting us be the judges of the truth of what you say?"

"Suppose," Ray said, glancing at Joe. "Suppose we said we just arrived in 1999 from the past in a time machine? Would you accept that as a starter?"

"No," Craig said bluntly.

"Then there's no use in our talking," Ray said.

"You mean you refuse to talk?" Craig asked softly.

"No, I don't refuse to talk," Ray said half angrily. "I just mean that anything we say will have to start from that, and if you refuse to believe that, it's no use talking."

"Wait a minute, Craig," Neal Smith spoke up. "Take a look at their clothes. They're the same kind of cloth as some that used to be up in the attic at home when I was a kid. They belonged to my grandfather."

Craig felt of the lapel of Joe's suit. He examined the buttons thoughtfully.

"They do look like clothes worn about fifty or so years ago, although the cut is modern—but styles repeat themselves. They would have to be before the zoot-suit era of 1960 to 1975, though, because with the reversion of styles the new plasticloth came in. Just the same, if they are spies their clothes don't mean a thing. The Varg Thrott could duplicate them and make it look authentic."

"That's right," Neal agreed. "It comes back to what we thought when Val told us about these guys. They can't do us any good, and it's safer for all of us if we get rid of them. Why run chances?"

"Why be hasty?" Val Nelson spoke up. "Let's take them to—you know who—and let him decide? He can put them under a lie detector and find out the truth."

"Not necessarily," Craig said skeptically. "They could have had their lies planted by hypnosis, so they actually believed them to be true. But you're right. We'd better pass this problem on higher up the ladder and let someone else take the responsibility for killing them."

"You're sure cold-blooded about it," Joe Ashford said. "I don't think I'm going to like you guys at all—especially if you kill us."

The three men smiled.

"Would you mind telling us something?" Joe asked, taking their smiles as a good sign. "Just what is this all about—this Varg Thrott, spy screens, and you fellows with your 'higher ups' and your being so cautious you want to kill us to play safe?"

"That don't work," Neal Smith said sharply. He pulled out a soft hollow tube and pointed it at Joe Ashford. "I'm beginning to see what you're up to. You have a signal generator on you, and right now you're stalling until the police can triangulate and locate us. Get going."

Val Nelson and Craig Blanning had stepped back as Neal Smith spoke. Now they were also holding short tubes. From the way they were held and pointed it was obvious they were some sort of dangerous weapon.

Ray Bradley closed one eye and studied the one pointed directly at his head. He could see through it. There seemed nothing inside it except some crosshairs toward the opposite end. Whatever it was, it was something that had not yet been invented in 1950—or even hinted at.

"Nuts," Joe was saying, disgustedly. "We're not moving until we get ready to. What harm would it do for you to answer my questions?"

"Just give the police time to locate us," Neal said. "Get moving."

His fist tightened around the tube in his hand. Nothing seemed to happen; but suddenly Joe felt his muscles cramping painfully. The sensation passed almost as soon as it began.

"Get going," Neal said tonelessly. "Next time I'll give you half strength instead of quarter—and don't tell me you don't know what this is…"

Joe hesitated briefly, then went to the door, now very meek and subdued. It was not a nice thing to feel your muscles starting to cramp.

It took an hour of crouched-over walking in the round concrete pipe under the streets to reach their next destination. This time they went downward instead of up to street level. It was a sub-basement area of unknown extent.

Ray and Joe were led part way down a corridor that extended much farther, and ushered into a room twelve by fourteen, with a twelve foot ceiling. There were chairs to sit down in. Other than that the room was bare.

Craig and Val stood over them with drawn weapons while Neal Smith knocked discreetly on a door leading into another room. A male voice on the other side called for him to enter. He put away his tube weapon and opened the door just far enough to slip through.

He was gone fifteen minutes before he returned to order Joe and Ray brought in. He took out his weapon. The three weapons covered Ray and Joe warily as they went into the next room.

The floor here was covered by a thick rug. There was an all metal desk. Behind the desk sat a man with iron gray hair and the look of an important man about him. He was regarding them worriedly as they came in.

His eyes dropped to two glasses laying on the desk, Ray's and Joe's eyes followed his gaze. The glasses were half full of water. Beside each, on a white paper napkin, was a small capsule, red in color with a bright yellow line around its center.

"I must ask you to take these," he said. "The alternative is the paralysis tube—which is very painful. The end result would be the same because we would give you the capsules when you were in a faint from the pain of the paralysis. All they are is a simple drug that will make you harmless, but not put you to sleep."

"A truth drug?" Ray asked. The man behind the desk nodded his head in the affirmative. "Good," Ray said, picking up the capsule and washing it down quickly. "Maybe you'll listen to us then and stop all this nonsense."

Joe reluctantly followed suit. Minutes later they were sprawled out in armchairs, barely able to hold up their heads.

Sometime later they were aware of a needle being stuck into their arm. Shortly after that they returned to full wakefulness.

"So you really are from the year 1950," the gray haired man said when they had recovered. "It seems incredible. By the way, I'm Arthur Granger. You could call me President of the United States, though that title is meaningless at present, and has been for the past ten years. The Vargians run things."

He held his hand out, first to Ray, then to Joe, and shook warmly. Val Nelson stood in the background, a friendly smile on his face. Neal Smith and Craig Blanning were relaxed in stiff armchairs near by. Neal caught Ray's eye.

"We checked on the building where your machine was," he said calmly. "It's like you described to us. You see, we couldn't accept even the story you told under a truth drug. We had to question you until we found something we could check. So after I found that building and its peculiar field, I went down to the library and hunted back through magazines of that period, from 1950 to 1955. There was quite a write-up in one of the big picture magazine weeklies of 1951 showing the same building and the same distortions, optical and gravitational. It made quite a story: two mysterious men rent the place and pay three months' rent in advance, who work in secrecy building something, who vanish, leaving behind a strange thing that is beyond the ability of science to explain. It all checks out."

"What else did it tell?" Joe asked.

Neal shrugged his shoulders. "Nothing much."

"We didn't check any further on your story," Arthur Granger said hastily. "We thought, after we had ascertained you were telling the truth that it would be more courteous to wait until you were free agents again."

"That's nice of you," Ray said dryly. "Now, if it isn't taking unfair advantage of you, suppose you tell us about this Varg Thrott and the Vargian police, and what that third eye in their foreheads is?"

"I don't blame you for being a trifle sore about the whole thing," Arthur Granger said. "When you learn the whole story you will understand our caution. But suppose we go to the dining hall and relax over some refreshments while we talk."

CHAPTER FIVE

"BACK AS EARLY AS 1948," Arthur Granger began, after he had played the host and provided several cans of beer from a wall dispenser, "there were eye witness accounts of strange craft in the skies. They received the name, flying saucers. In 1949 the government issued a paper, which admitted that they were real craft of some sort. One of your columnists, Walter Winchell, insisted they were guided missiles from the potential enemy, Russia. No doubt you know all this, since those years are just yesterday to you."

"Of course," Ray replied.

"The mysterious sky visitors continued to appear off and on during the succeeding twenty years," Granger continued. "Occasionally some pilot got too near one—and his plane went out of control and blew up mysteriously, as if it had suddenly changed into some high explosive. Other than these minor incidents of destruction there was no indication either of the nature or of the ultimate intent of the so-called flying saucers.

"During those years the United States Government spent considerable time and study on the mystery, even attempting to shoot them down when there was an opportunity. Nothing ever came of it. Several times anti-aircraft shells were photographed as they actually penetrated the strange craft, but each time, unaccountably, the shells passed right through them to explode farther up in their trajectories—even though they had proximity fuses that would explode them if they came within five feet of a flying sparrow."

"Is that the truth?" Ray exclaimed, startled. "Then that would mean that the craft were not material…"

"They were material, all right," Arthur Granger replied. "But, to go on with the story, I suppose it was inevitable that sooner or later we would bring one of the things down with a lucky shot. That was in September, 1976. The huge craft came plummeting down just outside Oklahoma City at dawn on September thirteenth. The crash was heard miles away—and that was natural, because the craft was nearly half a mile in diameter and a hundred yards thick at its center.

"There were corpses strewn all through the wreckage. They were corpses of men and women such as no one had ever suspected to exist. They appeared human in every last respect, except for the third eye in the forehead.

"In forty-eight hours thousands of scientists and technicians had converged on the spot. Metallurgists were sampling the materials of construction of the craft. Doctors were searching desperately for some sign of a spark of life somewhere in that three hundred acres of death and destruction. Five thousand state militia were keeping out the idle curiosity seekers, but even so the huge ship was melting under the stealthy depredations of souvenir hunters.

"Trucks were hauling off the dead—to take them to laboratories all over the world for study and dissection. There were two thousand dead Vargians—though no one knew at the time that they were Vargians, nor where they came from.

"In two months time every scrap of writing or printing in that wreck had been photographed, every circuit in wires or plumbing had been traced down, every piece of equipment had been dissected and studied.

"The world's greatest minds concentrated on the problem of resolving the mystery of the flying discs and nothing came of it. There was even uncertainty over the findings of the dissectors in the laboratories. They couldn't find the function of the third eye. They couldn't be sure whether the strange race was or was not related to the human, or just a product of convergent evolution of the type that brings two unrelated species close together in physical form and many of the elements of body construction and function.

"They weren't even able to determine how the huge ship could fly. There wasn't enough power generation equipment in it to lift a small passenger plane of that era, let alone a few hundred thousand tons of men and metal.

"Eventually most of those who had worked on the thing went back to their former pursuits, and gradually the ship dropped into the back pages of the newspapers. Three years after it had dropped from the sky the giant ship was taken over by a metal salvage company, which cut it up and loaded it onto flatcars destined for the smelters.

"Once in a while some writer would write an article speculating on the function of that third eye. He would review the findings of the surgeons—that its lens apparently had its focal plane on the surface of the brain itself, rather than an optical cortex; that it couldn't possibly co-ordinate with the two normal eyes, nor, apparently, turn in its socket, since it didn't have a socket. But always the conclusions of the various writers were the same—that it would be impossible to find out anything definite until and unless a living specimen were found.

"Thus things stood when, on the morning of May 5th in 1982, the Vargians made their first beachhead in Chicago. There was no warning. One moment the nine million people of the Chicago area were going their individual ways intent on their own business. The next they were groveling in torture or fainting outright from the effects of giant paralysis projectors far above in the sky.

"Before the sun set that day there were a million Vargians in Chicago. When the paralysis rays were shut off the Vargians were in complete control.

"The succeeding three months were undoubtedly the most unique in all history. Assuming the Government could have shot an atom bomb into the enemy concentration and destroyed it, it dared not do so because that same act would destroy nine million American citizens.

"The Government tried sending in troops and tanks and armored cars. There was a paralysis screen that completely circled the area. The screen would retreat whenever it was penetrated, to allow the soldiers to recover and retreat with their equipment.

"Peace delegations were sent into Chicago to talk with the Vargians. They were allowed to enter, they were gravely listened to, and then sent back where they came from without an answer.

"They carried stories with them of construction going on inside the city, of a scared but quiet populace going about its business 'as usual.' And the flow of industry through Chicago picked up and went on as normal as before that had all happened. A man in Seattle could still send a letter to Chicago and order and get a book or a radio or a new suit. A rancher could still send his cattle to the Chicago stockyards and get a check on a Chicago bank that would be honored and bring him his money. The Vargians went about their business of consolidating without any attempt to take over the reins of local government, and with no apparent desire to expand their beachhead nor even to state their terms with the United States Government. At all points their defenses were perfect. It was impossible to dislodge them.

"They ignored the populace except that they immediately set up a rigid exchange system. No one could leave the Chicago area unless someone came in to replace him. No train could leave unless one was at the same time coming in—and with the same number of cars. And the people in Chicago had to be fed, and the Vargians made no effort to feed them.

"Three months, and things were adjusted. The Vargians, talking to no one, stayed and built their buildings. One writer of that period, making a visit to Chicago, said, 'It gives one the feeling of a man about whom a huge Boa has wrapped its coils, as the snake gently arranges its body more comfortably, careful not to crush nor hurt nor bruise—until it is ready to constrict its coils with bone crushing strength.' And that's the way it was. Because of the nine million hostages the government was helpless. Because of the paralysis beam for which no defense could be found (though the Vargians evidently had one since they were unaffected by their own weapon), counter-invasion was impossible. For the same reason air invasion was impossible, and the few experimental attempts to bluff the Vargians with a show of air strength only met with tragic destruction of the airplanes before they were over the city.

"At the end of the first three month period a new phase materialized. Suddenly the Vargians took over the telephone exchanges and began using the telephone network to set up spy screens everyplace. They had set up housekeeping, and were now ready to look around, so to speak, and see how the insects that infested their house lived. They learned quickly, too. Where before they had made no attempt to talk, they now became quite conversational, gaining a rapid knowledge of language and everything connected with the human race. It became a common sight to see a dozen Vargians and as many people all in the reading room of the public library.

"The people took this as a hopeful sign. They went all out to make friends with the Vargians and show them that they would be excellent friends to have. The Vargians let them. But when the President tried to establish friendly relations with them they ignored all his advances with complete indifference.

"It was complete frustration. Complete. Impossible to describe. It was like trying to make friends with a stone, and then, attacking the stone for not being friendly, and then pleading with the stone to be friendly.

"They were completely indifferent. They left the displays of dissected and pickled Vargians from the wreck in the museums undisturbed. Even on the rare occasions when some fool shot a Vargian they merely took the corpse away and ignored the incident, not even asking the regular police force to hunt for the culprit. They did not kill—they paralyzed. If someone refused to obey their rare orders they gave him mild doses of paralysis until he obeyed. When he obeyed they left him alone.

"They could even be seen in the audiences in churches, gravely listening, saying nothing, going away as quietly and well behaved as they had come. One minister even spent his sermon period discussing the problem of whether Vargians had souls and a sense of the Presence of God, and the Vargians present listened attentively and without comment or expression.

"I've said they became quite conversational. That's true—about everything we human beings know; but even to this day no one has the slightest idea about where the Vargians came from, or anything else about them. They—"

"You mean," Ray Bradley interrupted, "that in seventeen years of occupation by the Vargians no one has ever gained the slightest clue as to their origin?"

"That's right," Arthur Granger said. The other three nodded their heads solemnly. "We have theories and ideas, of course. Books have been written discussing the origin of the Vargians." He smiled wryly. "Those books are read very avidly by the Vargians, and while they read them they never crack a smile or otherwise let on what reactions they get from our theorizing about them."

"What is the best theory you have on them?" Joe asked. "After all this time you must have one theory backed by sufficient evidence to make it sound better than any other."

"That's right," Arthur Granger agreed. "You'll remember I spoke about photographs of projectiles passing through them? Proximity fuses that a sparrow would touch off not being affected by the ships nor anything in them? From that has arisen the theory that they are from an adjacent three-space, and have found out how to travel into the fourth-space dimension and land in this three-space.

"But that theory has several disadvantages. In the first place, from an abstract point of analysis, traveling from rest in one mathematical plane to rest in another would be impossible, and the analogy of the planes carries over to the three-spaces, because our three-space and the one they would have come from would each be of no extent into the fourth dimension.

"There's another theory that seems more solid, though we have no experimental evidence to back *any* theory, as yet. You two men should know, since 1950 was the peak year of discovery in basic physics that matter itself exhibits many of the properties of light and other forms of radiant energy. In 1975 Jacobsen published his work demonstrating that the phenomenon of interference in wave mechanics reduced to equations, which when transformed by a velocity transformation, became laws of behavior of matter. In other words, waves packets traveling at velocities less than that of light relative to one another, behaved toward one another like matter.

"Right now, here in the underground, we have scientists working night and day trying to develop that starting point into a theory that the Vargians come from a realm of matter co-existent with our own in space, but of different frequency, and that in some way they are able to alter the frequency of their matter—and thus materialize into our wave band, or dematerialize back into their own native frequency. We haven't had much success—not any, really, except in the progress of the mathematics of the thing.

"But to get back to things; in 1984 the Vargians repeated their capture of Chicago in New York, Washington, Los Angeles, San Francisco, Portland, New Orleans, and Seattle. There wasn't anything to it. Already the Government and the world's top minds had exhausted every line of investigation of the problem, and the people were and had for a long time been told that there was no way of resisting the Vargians if they decided to expand their hold.

"The few uprisings against them were short lived. The Washington Government, having realized the inevitability of things, did the only thing it could do. It built such underground systems as it could, this one you have seen here being one of them. Beginning in the fall of '82 and up to the summer of '84 public works money poured into the construction of the concrete tubes under most of the major unoccupied cities, and sub-basements and other underground spaces were converted into livable quarters, so that at least the scientists could have some place to carry on the work of nibbling at the problem of how to eventually get rid of the Vargians.

"So you can understand our carefulness. Today, except in such places as this, all research work is constantly supervised by the Vargians."

"I see they have police now," Joe commented. "I suppose that means they have taken over the government and the judiciary too?"

"Yes," Arthur Granger said. "That took place in 1994. And today our biggest concern is the growing group of people who are convinced we are better off under the Vargians, and who brand us, the underground, as subversives and outlaws, and would give away our secret places if they could learn of them.

"And now we come down to the present. Starting suddenly two weeks ago, on May third, the Vargians showed signs of being very concerned and anxious about something. It had us mystified. They sent dozens of patrols out every day, investigating every slightest unusual incident. They would round up dozens of people and question them, and even hold some of them for days.

"Until you told us of your telephone conversation from the year 1950 we had no inkling of the cause."

"Yeah," Ray Bradley said, chuckling. "It was funny, I set my device for the end of the century and dialed a number, and a man answers and tells me the time and the date, then asks me what the date is I'm calling from, so I told him."

"What you, of course, didn't suspect," Val Nelson spoke up, "was that the Vargian that answered the phone knew you were telling the truth because all phones now have viewscreens that bring the image of the caller, and they can't be cut out on a call."

"Well, Ray," Joe said, "I guess your dream life is shattered. Your Nelva is undoubtedly a Vargian."

"Nelva?" Arthur Granger said. His face turned pale. He tried to speak, but his lips trembled.

"Where did you hear of Nelva?" Neal Smith asked tensely. "And what makes you call her a Vargian?"

CHAPTER SIX

QUICKLY Ray told the whole story, starting with the telephone calls, made so he could calibrate the controls of his invention for contacting other-time energy patterns in a wire, of the voice in his mind warning him out of the building seconds before the explosion, and of the subsequent dream in which that voice called itself Nelva.

As he talked Arthur Granger became more and more agitated. When he finished the man questioned him, had him repeat parts of the story. Then he did a strange thing. He covered his face with the palms of his hands and sobbed, his shoulders shaking, heartbroken sounds coming from his lips.

Ray and Joe watched this spectacle, amazed. Craig Blanning said in an undertone rumble, "Nelva is Mr. Granger's daughter. She was taken away from him by the Vargians when she was seventeen years old—five years ago."

Arthur Granger gained control of himself with an effort.

"I—I haven't had any news of her since they took her away," he said. "I didn't know whether she was alive or dead—or which would be the worse for her to be—until now."

"But why?" Ray asked. "I had gathered from what you said that the Vargians weren't interested in things like that."

"No one knows," Val Nelson spoke up. "So far as is known they haven't taken more than a dozen human beings into their buildings; and there was no cause for the ones they did take, so far as is known. With Nelva there certainly couldn't have been. She was beautiful for a girl of seventeen—but no more so than dozens of other girls. At the time we thought it might be because her father was the president-by-appointment of the underground, and that they would use her as a threat to force him to turn on us; but they never contacted him—never molested him. Every attempt we've made to find out something about what happened to her has met with a blank wall of silence. Until now."

There was a deep silence. Each of them was deep in his own private thoughts. Finally Joe Ashford broke the silence, almost timidly.

"One thing that struck me at the time," he said, "how could she speak to you directly in your mind from the future? I've thought a lot about it. Not many people can read minds. There's no use saying she did it through the circuit you had hooked into the telephone, Ray, because she contacted you later when you were asleep—after that circuit was blown up. And remember what she said? She said, 'Varg Thrott can trace me back and locate me,' or something like that. Just what was it she said, Ray?"

"She said, 'Varg Thrott can trace my thoughts back to me from you,'" Ray said slowly, "and as I remember it, it seemed not so much that she was afraid Varg Thrott would find where she was, as that he or it would find out it was she who was contacting me and had saved my life. And who is Varg Thrott? Their ruler?"

"No," Neal Smith said. "Thrott is the equivalent of the English 'territorial government' and Varg is of course what they call themselves, like our term, American. So the Varg Thrott is the collective Vargian population."

"And that three-eyed female whose picture is in the spyscreen in the drugstore?" Joe asked. "I was thinking Varg Thrott was her name. Who is she?"

"As nearly as we can gather," Neal answered, "she is their queen or ruler. She must be something like that because her picture is plastered all over the country."

"So Nelva is in the hands of the Vargians," Ray Bradley said softly.

Joe looked intently at Ray, his eyes softening at what he saw there. He looked up at Arthur Granger and winked cheerfully.

"If the Vargians only knew it," he said brightly, "they're in for a hard time of it. You don't know what a sly and devious mind lurks behind those eyes of his. Once he sinks his mental teeth into anything he never lets go."

Ray didn't seem to hear what Joe said. His eyes were half closed, his fingers toying with the empty glass in his hand.

"He looks that way now," Val Nelson said. "I'd almost say he looks sinister."

"He doesn't hear a word you are saying," Joe said with a broad smile.

After an interval of silence Ray's eyes shot open. "Is there such a thing as a map of the city? If you have one, bring it to me."

"I have one in my desk," Arthur Granger said. "Also maps of other cities and of the whole country, right up to date."

"Just bring the one of the city," Ray said brusquely. Mr. Granger hesitated, then rose and left the room. Shortly he returned with a folded map. Ray took it and spread it open on the floor. Joe got down beside him and studied the map.

There seemed practically no changes in the city. The general street layout was still the same. There was a generous sprinkle of red blocks on the map.

"Those red places," Arthur Granger volunteered, "are the Varg Thrott—offices and residential sections. It's against the law for us to trespass where the red squares are."

Ray Bradley nodded his head, his eyes scanning the map. Suddenly he grunted in satisfaction. Then his eyes moved to another part of the map and studied it minutely.

Joe divided his attention between the map and Ray. He guessed what was on Ray's mind, but said nothing, leaving it up to Ray to decide what to say.

Finally Ray stood up and folded the map together. When he spoke his voice was quite casual.

"I think," he said absently, "that the first thing is for us to get acquainted with things as they are now—get around a bit, and learn to pass as ordinary citizens." He smiled briefly. "Joe and I gawked so much at all the sights that we stood out like a couple of hillbillies on their first visit to New York."

"Do you think—"

Arthur Granger's expression was one of pleading and suffering, Ray Bradley's eyes softened.

"All I can say," he answered the unvoiced question, "is that—I want to find Nelva as much as you do. Is that enough?"

Ray and Joe were back in their hotel room. Val Nelson had led them back through the concrete tubes under the streets. The door had just closed behind him. They were finally alone.

"So you think Nelva is in that red spot where our office used to be," Joe said softly.

"I thought you read my mind on that," Ray said calmly. "It stands to reason. I began to realize it while we were building the time travel machine. The coil setup in that was designed to be powerful enough to pull itself and the whole machine through time. The coil group in that first setup was small, designed merely to pull insignificant electric currents out of their time co-ordinate, I asked myself the question, how could Nelva reach across half a century of time into the past and unerringly contact my mind alone?"

"I didn't think of that until I saw you looking at that red square on the map in the spot where we had our office," Joe said. "It came to me then. Your gadget must have been instruments in bridging the gap."

"That's right," Ray said. "Its effects were greater than I realized. She must have been standing so that her brain was actually in the field. It in some way made her aware of what was going on. She must have special abilities along the lines of telepathy anyway, and once the coil-bridge across time established contact between her mind and mine it was possible for her to reach me the second time."

"Do you think she will contact you now that we're here?" Joe asked.

"I don't know," Ray said thoughtfully. "You know, a lot of things are beginning to perk in my mind. Why did the Vargians come? What is their object in staying? Power? They don't seem to especially relish the job of occupying the United States. We didn't ask, but I seemed to gather that they weren't exploiting us in any way. Colonizers usually start stripping the country they conquer of its wealth and ship it back home.

"But if not power or wealth, what? Knowledge? That might have been, but we can discount that, because their only curiosity about our science and history seems to have been for the purpose of understanding us well enough to manage us successfully. I doubt if the motive for their occupation is to steal our knowledge. A lightning raid on a bookstore by a small band of them would have given them that without the necessity of occupying the whole country.

"What then? Does that kidnapping of Nelva and a few others mean anything? Or did they just pick up random specimens, or perhaps pets that struck the fancy of some female of their species?"

"I wonder if they have the secret of time travel?" Joe asked.

"I've thought about that, too," Ray said. "I think they must have. Consider the explosion. A time travel bomb of some sort could have been the cause of that explosion that wrecked our office and lab. Certainly no energy those coils could carry would have blown it up. But that brings up another question. Why did they want to kill us?"

"Obviously," Joe said, "because we have the knowledge of time travel, and they don't want us to give that knowledge to the human race."

"Obviously," Ray agreed. "It's also obvious that we didn't give it out up to now, or it would be common knowledge to these people. As it is, they had never heard of it."

"That gives us the motive for them trying to kill us," Joe said. "But what's in back of that?"

"Consider this," Ray said. "Suppose that instead of coming from another space, or instead of their changing the frequency of their matter, they actually come from another time? What if they are our descendants—a million years from now?"

CHAPTER SEVEN

RAY BRADLEY and Joe Ashford were awakened in the morning by a knock at the door. Ray called out that he was coming as he slid out of bed. He was halfway to the door before he was fully awake."

"Who is it?" he asked sharply, coming to an abrupt stop.

"It's me," a low voice said. "Val Nelson."

Ray opened the door quickly and let him in.

"I brought you some clothes," Val said from behind his armload of boxes. "All modern. It wouldn't do for you to be picked up with 1950 vintage sox on, you know."

"That's right," Ray smiled. "Our clothes would give us away."

Joe rolled over and opened one sleepy eye, closed it in thought, then opened it again. He sat up and yawned widely then planted his feet on the floor and stood up.

"Hi, Val," he yawned, stretching and scratching, his mussed up head. "What's cookin' outside?"

"The Varg Thrott is trying awfully hard to find you," Val said lightly. "They've blocked off the streets around that drug store and taken down the wall in back of the telephone booths."

"Then they'll find the tunnel into the street," Ray said.

"I don't think so," Val said. "They'll find the first door leading into the other wall, and the place where we went down into the basement. From there they'll find the very obvious avenue of escape into the alley by the basement steps and assume that's the way you went. We're hoping they'll come to the conclusion that if you were the two they were looking for, you wouldn't have had time to know about secret doors in the back of telephone booths. By the way, you didn't, did you?"

"No," Ray said. "We were going to try to find the address of that telephone number we called and start looking from there for some trace of Nelva."

"That's really all you came into your future for, wasn't it?" Val said, looking queerly at Ray.

Ray shrugged. "Perhaps," he said. "Maybe half of it was to try out the time travel machine. Did I tell you fellows that it was Nelva who told me how to build it?"

"No," Val exclaimed. "That means she knew then."

"Not necessarily," Ray said. "She asked me first to describe my hookup. That could have been to find out—or to make sure I knew what I had done rather than stumbled onto it by some freakish circumstance."

Val relaxed in the lone armchair in the room while Ray and Joe bathed and dressed in the new clothes. The styles weren't much different than their old clothes, but the materials were vastly different to the touch.

"The Vargians have let us develop pretty much undisturbed," Val said conversationally. "Aside from their ever-present spy screens—which we can never know are operating or not operating, by the way—they stay away from us except in cases like the present where they have to interfere for some reason. I've brought you some money. Not too much, but there's plenty more when it's gone.

"Also, I've instructions to tell you that we are all to cooperate with you two in every way. There'll always be someone within view of you. Dig into your ear with your little finger when you want to know something, and shortly after someone will stop and talk with you. Whoever it is, you can be sure it is one of us."

"And who, exactly, are you?" Joe asked, smiling. "I didn't get that quite straight last night."

"We're the heirs of government," Val said seriously. "The Government at Washington realized that the Vargians were going to eventually take over the whole country. They figured that sooner or later the human race would find a way to fight them successfully, and when that time came there should be some sort of historical continuity of authority to take over. We call ourselves the Custodians."

Ray and Joe inspected themselves critically in the dresser mirror and marveled how styles had come back to those of 1950 so exactly in 1999. Or perhaps they had never changed.

"The latest styles," Val grinned. "Two years ago you would have stood out like two lights in the dark if you had walked down the street in your own clothes."

Breakfast was something new and surprising. There was a thick purple juice that tasted like meat, three capsules, and perfectly brewed coffee. The capsules, Val explained, were an expanding gelatin that would provide exactly the right amount of solid for good health.

Everything had come from coin operated vending machines in a cafeteria. There was nothing so surprising about that, but it was the flavors of things that was the surprise. Especially the coffee. Val Nelson couldn't explain that.

"Maybe our sense of taste was altered in coming here," Joe suggested.

"No," Ray said. "How about yesterday? Things tasted normal then. It must be something they add that brings out the full flavor."

After breakfast Val conducted them on a tour of the city. If they had not seen the three-eyed men at the entrance to the drugstore the day before they might have found it hard to believe they existed. None were in sight anywhere, though in almost every place they went they encountered the three dimensional color pictures of the Vargian queen—if that was what she was. There was something compelling—hypnotic—about her beauty. That third eye sleeping in the center of her forehead became, after a while, something more normal than a smooth one. The dualism of emotion expressed on her face did not so much hint at a dual personality as a breadth of personality. And Ray Bradley noticed that that face seemed to exercise the same attractive force on all others. Almost no one seemed able to pass that color picture within which lurked a spyscreen without looking up at it intently.

There were police, but they were ordinary humans. Val explained that most of the routine police work was in the hands of the people—under close direction of the Vargians.

It wasn't until almost noon that Val took them to a large department store and they saw their first Vargian at close hand.

It was a female Vargian. Except for her third eye, which was disappointingly more like a tumor than an eye, she might have passed for an exceptionally tall, ordinary woman. She was all of six feet three inches tall, but with such a perfectly proportioned figure under her trim clothes that at a distance she seemed almost small. Near at hand as she brushed by Ray and Joe, there was something breathtaking about her.

She didn't notice them. Her mind was obviously wrapped up in her shopping. Under her arm was a suit box. Her eyes roamed over the heads of the many people in the store, looking for some department she had in mind.

After she had gone Joe looked amusedly at Val and whispered, "Do, you mean to tell me there has been no inter-marrying of Vargians and humans?"

"That's right," Val asserted.

"All I have to say," Joe said, "is that the repulsion must all be on the Vargian side. I could go for that babe without any encouragement at all."

"Don't try it," Val said. "I've seen it tried." He refused to elaborate on that.

As the day wore on they covered a large part of the city. Ray and Joe were quickly learning the customs and habits that were necessary to life in 1999. It was a unique experience—entering city life after a half-century jump. It descended from the heights of the bizarre by successive stages to the commonplace. The succession of surprises gradually dulled the ability to become surprised at anything.

On every hand they saw commonplace things after half a century of development and style change. Two things impressed them more than any others.

There were no irons nor ironing machines. They learned from Val Nelson that the plastics used in clothes returned to their carefully pressed state on washing in hot water, so that ironing had become a thing of the past.

That was understandable. Certain plastics even back in 1950 had been known to have what came to be known as "form memory," and however distorted or pulled out of shape, under certain conditions they would resume the shape they had previously held.

The second thing was totally unexpected and incomprehensible. The electric fan had neither blades nor motor nor any other moving part. It consisted of an ornamental grill atop a heavy base, with a light cord. When turned on air rushed through the grill under the impetus of some strange and unseen force—air that was cool and refreshing, and came in a strong blast when the switch was on full, or barely drifted when it was on low.

Other things, the invisible radiophones that were worn in the ear and were both transmitters, and receivers, the three dimensional color movies in broad daylight, the combination radios that had television recorders that took a television program on a wire spool for later playback just as it did sound, were delightful surprises—but expected.

And at last the day ended. Ray and Joe found themselves alone in their room once more, physically and emotionally exhausted, but confident that they could go forth on their own without mishap from now on.

They were to learn later that their every move in public had been noted and watched, and that even now, in the security of their room, their slightest action and word was being observed by several Vargians across the city in an office that occupied the same space as their office that had been destroyed as they rushed from it, back in 1950.

CHAPTER EIGHT

VAL NELSON paused outside the door to Ray's and Joe's room as he closed it, his eyes speculatively on the blank door panel. Then he left the hotel, his footsteps purposeful and hurried.

He caught a bus at the corner. Several blocks later he transferred to another bus. When he got off he walked unhurriedly until he came to an alley. Just before he reached it he casually surveyed the street to make sure the few pedestrians in sight were not noticing him.

As he came even with the alley he darted in. It was dark here. Not dark enough yet to be black, but enough so that he could be sure no one glancing down the alley from the street would be able to see him.

He paused in a doorway, getting his bearings, then carefully counted his measured steps along the building walls, his hands lightly trailing along the wall surface to guide him. When he stopped he felt around carefully until his fingers told him he had found the right brick.

From his pocket he took a small bit of permanently magnetized metal and touched it to the brick. Inside there was a faint click. The magnet in Val's fingers had attracted a small bit of iron inside the brick, causing it to swing forward and close a contact that connected a hidden phone to a private wire. Concealed under the false brick front was a microphone pickup and a small loudspeaker, so that after the connection was made he could speak to the blank wall in a low voice and also hear the soft-spoken replies. When he finished and removed the magnet metal the connection would be broken.

"Yes?" a voice vibrated from the wall with bare audibility. It was a deep, cavernous voice—but the quality of that voice might have been altered by the effects of the brick sounding board.

"Nelson," Val said briefly.

"No further instructions," the cavernous voice said. "There is an eavesdropper installed in their room in the usual place. Please check to make sure it is not discovered. You're excused."

Val put the magnet back in his pocket and returned to the street. Two blocks further on he casually entered a public lavatory, deposited a nickel in a coin slot, and entered a stall. Seconds later the "occupied" notice slipped around to "unoccupied" without the door having been opened. This was one of the many entrances into the underground network of passages and rooms of the Custodians.

He had squeezed through a narrow opening in the back wall of the stall onto an elevator that dropped slowly as soon as he had shut the panel. When the elevator stopped a door opened. He stepped out into Arthur Granger's private office.

Besides the gray haired president of the Custodians, Neal Smith and Craig Blanning were there. From the expressions on their faces at Val's coming, they had been waiting for some time.

He grinned at them and made an O with thumb and finger. "Everything's set," he said.

"Then the Vargians acted on your suggestion to give them a free hand for the present?" Neal asked.

"Right," Val said, sitting on the edge of the desk. "I just reported to them through the alley phone contact and was told there'd be no further instructions tonight, but to check and make sure Ray and Joe hadn't discovered the eavesdropper they put in their room."

He looked at Arthur Granger with admiration tinged with something else.

"That was a very good act you put on about Nelva being your daughter," he said. "It should keep them in line unless Nelva manages to contact Ray Bradley again by telepathy."

"It was easy," Arthur Granger said, trying to squelch a smile that rose against his will. "Hiding my face with my hands made it simple."

"It almost convinced me," Val said, giving Arthur a keen glance. "Are you sure it isn't true?"

Arthur shrugged in disdain. "Are you relying on facts now?" he asked. "If you are you're no use to us."

"That's right," Val Nelson said woodenly. "I must consider both alternatives in my reactions—just as you must consider always the possibility of my being a traitor."

"What do you think of Ray and Joe?" Neal Smith asked. "You've been with them all day."

"They're all they claim," Val said. "That's obvious. They come from the age of direct thinkers. In 1950 they had codes. Codes of honesty. Codes of integrity. They did most of their reacting on trust and faith. Pragmatism was just a crude abstraction. Dialectical materialism was being practiced by a few fools in Russia with their brains clouded by a sense of success. The third leg of the triangle of modern Tactics, going under the grandiose title of non-Aristotelian logic, was fumbling along on the premise that man merely imitates the animals, and trying to create a cult. I doubt if the actual processes of reasoning of today would occur to Ray and Joe, let alone occur to them as a matter of course."

"It's refreshing to know them," Craig Blanning said lazily. "They're like children. They stumble onto something and play around at telephones with it. Then they come into the future to rescue the damsel in distress like in some dated story book." His eyes held a mixture of liking and respect. "I'll bet they'd die under torture before they'd reveal this hiding place—if it came right down to it."

"They're knights in shining armor, all right," Val said, smiling. "In fact, they'd probably come to the conclusion we weren't for them if they learned the Vargians know all about us and that we know the Vargians know all about us. They would be unable to understand the complexities of the present situation. They'd cease to trust us. They'd become confused."

"Or," Neal Smith said softly, "they'd make us look like amateurs. They'd catch us unawares. They'd be licked until the last instant—and come out on top."

"They're going to come out on top anyway," Arthur Granger said.

"*You* know the way I mean," Neal said.

"Yes," Arthur said, his face becoming strained. "I know. We all do. So do the Vargians. Strange, how events can focus until everything, past and future, hangs on one insignificant event—like Ray finding Nelva."

CHAPTER NINE

RAY LAY WIDE-AWAKE listening to the soft snores of Joe, his eyes staring at the gloom of the ceiling. When he closed his eyes signs gyrated before them and window dummies went through motions, so he kept them open.

He felt restless. For a while he thought it must be due to the nervousness of encountering so many new things in one day and trying to keep up with them. He got up once and bathed his eyes in warm water. The procession of novelties grew less irritating in the dark of the room; but the restlessness grew worse, if anything.

He switched his thoughts to Nelva. So Arthur Granger was her father. That was something. It meant that he could be sure of help from that quarter.

Nelva would be twenty-one or two-three at the most. That was nice. It would have been a letdown if she were forty. And she was an ordinary human. It would have been horrible if she had turned out to be one of the three-eyed people like that girl who was queen of the Vargians.

He closed his eyes and tried to call her mentally, not really expecting her to answer, disappointed because she didn't. Could she sense his mental voice? Was she silent because it would be too dangerous for her to answer his call? He wished he knew.

His restlessness increased. He wondered if it would be much of a risk to walk off his restlessness. He looked over at Joe and decided there was no use waking him. He dressed in the dark, keeping quiet.

At the door he decided he'd better leave a note in case Joe woke up and missed him. He closed the door to a bare crack and stood under a light in the hall while he scribbled the note. He wrote: Have gone for walk. If I don't return lay low until rendezvous with the time machine. Keep quiet.

He slipped it through the crack in the door halfway up and saw it land, a ghostly rectangle on the dark rug. Then he carefully closed and locked the door. At the desk in the lobby he gave the night clerk the key and mumbled he would be back shortly.

The air had cooled with the night. The sky was clear and dotted with a myriad of stars. He held his head up, watching them, feeling that in some way they linked him with the past.

There was the north star, Polaris. It took fifty years for light from it to reach the Earth. The light from it that was striking his eyes had left it about the time he had left the past and plunged forward into the future.

Time and space were a strange mixture. The light from Polaris, for instance. In two weeks the time machine would return, and he could go back to 1950—and the light striking his eyes now would just be leaving Polaris—yet here it was.

In that simple fact was the clue to reality that had enabled him to build the time machine.

His feet had led him into a residential section. Every two blocks there were street lamps. In between were the dark hulks of houses and the shadowy clusters of shrubs, with here and there the gleam of reflected light from a parked car.

He became aware, finally, that he was being followed. He let this knowledge penetrate slowly. It could be a Vargian or a man. He decided it must be a man—one of the agents of the Custodians.

It irritated him somehow. Of course it was well intended, but they were a little too obliging if they kept a man outside the hotel all night just in case he decided to take a walk.

At the next streetlight he paused and casually put his little finger in his ear and made motions like he was trying to clean out his ear.

The footsteps, which had stopped when he stopped, sounded after a brief silence. A man moved into the dim light of the street lamp. It was Neal Smith.

"Why didn't you join me instead of following me?" Ray asked calmly.

"I thought perhaps you wanted to be alone," Neal said unabashed. "I could as easily have kept you from knowing you were being followed if I'd wanted to."

"I suppose you could have," Ray said, sizing up the trim figure of the Custodian man. "As a matter of fact, I suppose it was thoughtful of you not to barge in. I was restless and wanted to walk it off."

"I can drop back again," Neal suggested.

"No." Ray said, frowning. "The illusion of being alone wouldn't be there. I'd keep thinking of you back there, following me. Now that you're here, though I don't know why you should be, I'll be glad of your company. That is, if you don't mind."

"I'm sure it will be much more comfortable than lurking along behind," Neal said with a chuckle.

His eyes studied Ray Bradley covertly as they walked along in silence. He was trying to think of something he might say that would start the conversation rolling.

Ray's eyes were slightly downcast, unseeing except for almost unconscious guidance of his footsteps. He had all but forgotten Neal Smith.

It had come to him suddenly back there under the street lamp when Neal walked up. He knew suddenly why he was restless. That restlessness was an alarm signal from his subconscious. Not exactly an alarm signal either. His subconscious mind had run into a problem and was trying to work through to conscious thought.

The pattern was familiar to him. His mind generally worked that way. At least he thought it did. In his early introvertive studies of himself he had learned that facts had a way of sinking into regions of his mind where conscious thought didn't reach. There they put themselves together into logical thought, forcing themselves back into consciousness like an oxygen-starved swimmer striving to reach the surface from the depths.

It wasn't disciplined thinking. It was irrational, psychotic. Sometimes when it was all over and everything became clear he was amazed at its irrational complexity. An accidental factor would follow a succession of thought carried on by poetic analogy, humor, plain nonsense, until it arrived at a missing link in a train of serious thinking—the whole entirely subconscious, and it would burst into consciousness like a voice from some other world.

Now, as he walked along in the dark with Neal Smith beside him, he let his mind play idly on this, feeling that he was getting somewhere. He wasn't arriving at any conclusions. On the contrary, he felt strongly that there was some conclusion already reached about something, deep in his mind, and if he could only soothe his thoughts, lessen the nervous tension created by the frustration of his subconscious in its inability to bring forth that thought, it would come.

And suddenly it was there. The television wire recorder. It rose into his mind vividly. He looked at it without at first getting its import. Then he knew.

He and Joe had stood in front of the spyscreen for at least twenty seconds, startled by the picture of the Vargian queen. That had been noticed by whoever was watching through the 1999 edition of a television camera behind that screen. Undoubtedly their faces had been recorded.

He opened his mouth to tell Neal about it—then snapped it closed. Other thoughts were flooding to the surface now.

Surely Val Nelson would have been aware of the danger of them appearing in public—passing before other spyscreens? He should have warned them, perhaps given them some sort of disguise so their features would be different enough to not be recognized easily. Why hadn't he? Was it carelessness of thinking? None of these men of 1999 seemed to be careless thinkers.

More to the point, why hadn't the Vargians gone after him and captured him during the day? They undoubtedly could have.

But—of course all that hinged on the spyscreen being connected to a television wire recorder like that one in the department store the clerk had shown him while Val looked on. Or did it? It was almost as if Val Nelson had *known* the Vargians wouldn't have had a wire recorder ready to photograph him, or had known the Vargians wouldn't try to capture him and Joe just yet.

It didn't make sense. The Vargians wanted to kill him. They had had dozens of chances to capture him during the day. They probably even knew the number of his room at the hotel by now. Yet they left him alone. Did that mean they had changed their minds?

And if he, a newcomer to 1999 could see all this, it was certain Val Nelson had seen it. Maybe not Neal Smith. Maybe only Val, since Val was the only one who had actually seen them stand open mouthed before that spyscreen in the drug store.

The drug store! Val had said the Vargians had closed off the area and were tearing out the wall behind the telephone booth. If that were a lie...

"I'm getting tired of walking, Neal," Ray said. "Want to go on a bus ride with me? No. Don't tell me where to ride. I'd just like to catch the first bus that comes along and ride for a while and switch to another, and wind up at the hotel about the time I get sleepy, O.K.?"

"O.K.," Neal agreed. "The bus line's two blocks over. Oh. I keep forgetting that this is your town, even though it's fifty years away from your native time."

"I tend to forget it myself," Ray said. "But even bus routes don't change much after they're once laid out—and street names almost never."

The bus route had changed, however—which was a bit of luck. It took him to the street where the drugstore was. And there was another bit of luck. There were lights in the store. It was evidently an all night drug store.

The bus stopped to pick up several passengers. Ray had a full thirty seconds to study the interior of the store. There was no slightest sign of it being blocked off, or of any destruction back by the telephone booths.

Val Nelson had lied.

Ray Bradley wasn't as surprised at this as he was at his own reaction to the fact. Immediately his restless feeling disappeared.

Common sense would have prophesied that learning he could not believe those who seemed to be his friends should have plunged him into a feeling of insecurity. It didn't. It made him suddenly relaxed and sleepy.

The bus passed the side street where he had first arrived in this world of 1999. It was dark and deserted. It made him think back and recall that he hadn't told anyone where his time travel machine was. They hadn't asked him—and that, too, was strange. It would have been natural for Val and Neal and the other two to ask where the time travel machine was, and express the desire to see it. They hadn't, and that was why he hadn't thought to tell them.

Why hadn't they asked? Was it because they already knew? Or was it because time travel was so commonplace with them that they had ceased to be curious about it?

If Val was a traitor working with the Vargians, he might know about time travel, assuming the Vargians came from another time rather than another space—but then, if the others were the Custodians of Government, hiding from the Vargians, would they consider time travel so routine that they wouldn't think to be curious about his time travel machine?

Neal and Val, and also Arthur Granger and Craig Blanning, all were together on this. What, then, of Granger's claim to being Nelva's father? Was that, too, a lie?

Perhaps only Nelva herself could tell him that. Until she did he would have to assume it to be a lie—to assume that Arthur Granger was *not* her father.

The whole thing was becoming clear now. It only made sense if it were assumed that both the Custodians and the Vargians *wanted* him to look for and *find* Nelva—because they themselves didn't know where she was.

Or could it be that they didn't know *when* she was?

"I think I'm sleepy enough to go back to the hotel now, Neal," Ray said, yawning widely.

CHAPTER TEN

RAY AWAKENED to find Joe already up and dressed. His wristwatch said one o'clock. Val Nelson was there too. Val and Joe were over by the window talking in a low voice so as not to disturb him. He listened to them for a while.

"Good ol' Joe," Ray thought. "He doesn't have the slightest suspicion that we are prisoners already, in the hands of the Vargians."

He thought it over a bit more, deciding it would be wise to let things play along for the time being. Keep his suspicions and knowledge to himself. Even keep them from Joe. An honest and unsuspecting Joe would be his best defense for the present. In a tight spot Joe would follow his orders without question, and later on he could explain everything to him—when things broke wide open, as they surely would.

He yawned vocally and sat up.

"So you're finally awake," Joe said. "What do you mean, prowling around all night without me?"

"I had Neal Smith for company," Ray said sleepily. "Good company, too. Keeps his mouth shut instead of chattering like a monkey."

"No reflections on anyone present, I trust?" Joe laughed.

Val Nelson smiled quietly, remembering Neal's report that Ray had been restless and apparently on edge from trying to get in touch with Nelva via telepathy. The Vargian monitor on the snooperscreen watching the room had reported Ray to have come in and been asleep in five minutes.

"Get dressed," Val said. "Then we'll go down and Joe and I can have lunch while you eat breakfast."

"O.K.," Ray said willingly. "And after we eat I'd like to take a look at the outside of some of the Vargian sections of town. You'll be able to come along with us, won't you, Val?" He put an anxious note into his voice, though he knew that there was little possibility of Val *not* tagging along.

"Of course," Val said. "Mr. Granger has freed me from other duties so I could devote all my time to helping you two. By the way, this evening he wants to see you and have a long talk with you about your plans. Nelva hasn't contacted you yet, has she?"

"No," Ray said, putting a worried frown on his face for Val's benefit. "I've been trying—but I never had any previous experience with telepathy, so I don't know really how to go about it."

"I don't know any more about it than you do," Val said. "I've been thinking though—do you suppose there might have been some special condition present that first time that put your minds in tune with each other, and kept them that way long enough for the second successful attempt; but that it's gone now?"

"I'm beginning to think that," Ray said, giving himself a last inspection in the dresser mirror. "In fact, last night I came to the conclusion I would forget about the telepathy angle and concentrate on figuring out some way to get into the Vargian building where I think she's kept prisoner." He noticed the satisfied gleam that appeared for a split second in Val's eyes. "I'm ready. Let's go. I'm really hungry, too."

The bus they transferred to was one that would take them right through one of the Vargian residential sections, Val assured them as they boarded it. Before it reached that section it was half full of Vargians and ordinary people, sitting side by side.

There were even Vargian children on the bus: three long-legged ones around ten years old from human standards. Ray thought of long-legged colts he had seen on a farm once as he watched them. They had the same kind of leggy clumsiness, the same hint of future grace and proportion.

He covertly studied the Vargians sitting near him, trying to figure out the purpose of their third eye—detect some change or sign of expression in it; but in every Vargian it remained the same, filmed over in a semblance of sleep.

There was one Vargian woman sitting across the aisle two seats ahead whom he watched more than the others because he could do so with half closed eyes and without turning his head in obviousness. She, like all Vargians, sat tall and erect of body, her thinness rather attractive, her face very like that of any woman except for the wider forehead and the third eye.

As he watched, she unaccountably looked forward to the front entrance of the bus and smiled. Ray followed her glance and saw nothing. A moment later the bus pulled into the curb at a corner and stopped. Another Vargian woman got on, paid her fare, and came down the aisle with a smile on her face to sit beside the one Ray had been watching.

Could it be that that third eye was an extra-temporal organ of sight? Able to see a little way into the future? The woman had looked at the front of the bus as though she was actually *seeing* her friend *before* she had boarded the bus. He made a mental note to study the actions of the Vargians with that theory in mind.

Finally they were in the Vargian residential section. In the space of a few blocks the bus emptied its Vargians. On the sidewalks were only Vargians; grownups walking along or standing talking together, Vargian children playing games of hopskip, catch, and all the other varied games of childhood.

There was a Vargian policeman on a motorcycle, but in most of the cars that sped along the street were ordinary people.

Most of the houses were new, but here and there Ray recognized one that had been in place in 1950. He could tell by Joe Ashford's face that he recognized these familiar landmarks too.

They were coming to where the old office building had been. A skyscraper stood there now, visible from blocks away. Joe had seen it too.

They didn't talk. There was no need to. Each knew what was in the other's mind. As the bus stopped to disgorge most of the remaining Vargians and take on a few more, Ray stared up at the third floor windows in the space his own office had occupied forty-nine years before.

It would be from there that the time-travel bomb had been sent to destroy him. It was probably there that Nelva had stood when she first telepathed her warning that had saved them from the bomb.

The windows stared back at him without hint of expression. The bus started. Ray fought an impulse to jump up and leap off the bus at the next corner.

The Vargians knew he was there. They *must* know he was riding the bus and had been looking up at that third floor line of windows. But they were carrying on the pretense of not knowing, just as Val Nelson was carrying on the pretense of not being their guard and warden. Would that pretense be kept up any longer if he were to jump off the bus and try to reach those offices? Probably not.

What would happen, then, if he precipitated things? Would they carry on their pretense to its logical conclusion and pretend they had been looking for him—and kill him or imprison him?

Ray considered the possibility. It might be the only way of getting ahead in his search for Nelva. Or maybe at the underground office of Arthur Granger tonight they would give him a suggested line of action.

He decided to wait and see. Tomorrow he could still come here and precipitate things by a "foolish" impulse. But also, tomorrow a less foolish plan might be apparent. Also, there were new questions clamoring to be answered. Paramount among them was, how old was a Vargian at maturity? How long did they live before they became old? So far there had been no oldsters among the Vargians he had seen.

Several blocks beyond the Vargian residential section Ray saw a theater and all of them hastened to get off and look around.

They reached Arthur Granger's underground office at dinnertime. A table had been brought in and plates laid out in anticipation, Craig Blanning and Neal Smith were there also.

When Val Nelson brought them in he excused himself and was gone nearly half an hour. Ray wondered if he were reporting to the Vargians. He listened to Joe take the conversational ball and tell enthusiastically of the day's events, and was secretly glad he had left Joe in the dark as an innocent buffer against suspicion. It enabled him to enter the conversation with not much more than well placed facial expressions and an occasional word or two while studying the three listening to Joe's chatter.

Arthur Granger was quite definitely hamming it when he showed concern over his "daughter," Nelva. It was well done. Ray realized that if he had not been looking with suspicious eyes he would never have spotted it as deception.

He listened, and speculated on the connection between these men and the Vargians, and what role Nelva played in all this. The possibility had returned that she might be a Vargian herself, now that it was fairly certain Arthur Granger wasn't her father; but the prospect wasn't hideous any more. Vargian women lacked the sex appeal of a small woman, but what they lacked in petiteness they made up for in grace of bearing and intelligence.

Ray caught the sense of his thoughts and smiled at himself. He was falling for a pattern—boy rescues girl, boy marries girl. It probably wouldn't work out that way at all. He told himself that, but somewhere inside his mind his own voice called him a liar. It was too unthinkable to go into the future dramatically in a time machine and rescue a matron or an old woman. It was even more unthinkable to do the same and rescue a beautiful but happily married woman and have her husband thank them politely.

Val returned casually. It was a signal for them to begin eating. This time there were surprises. Fresh tomatoes and delicious steaks. They created in Ray a deep homesickness for his own age, 1950, trailing along behind this strange age of domination by the Varg Thrott, which apparently made the United States a colony of some unknown world peopled by Vargians.

He recalled what he had mentioned to Joe so long ago; that they might be still living in this age somewhere, and they could possibly drop in and see themselves as they would be at seventy-five years of age.

The idea took hold. Who, of all the people alive in 1999, could he and Joe trust implicitly? Only themselves. If they could find themselves—actually their physical selves—they could find out what it was all about.

Or could they? Suppose he could find Ray Bradley 75 and talk to him. Could Ray 75 tell him, Ray 25 that tomorrow he would do this and that, because he remembered doing it? If so, then Ray 75 could remember what he himself would be doing tomorrow because as Ray 25 he had watched him do it. That would make causes and effects entirely circular and repetitious. He would go through the coming events and go back to 1950 and living fifty years and go through them again as Ray 75 while another Ray 25 would go through the coming adventures. It would be perfectly circular—a juke box record being played over and over again. Denying the possibility of that might lead to some clue that would account for the fact that they couldn't just stop in any time they chose to as they came forward in time. Still—

"Tell me something," he spoke up. The others stopped talking to listen. "Are either Joe or I alive today and seventy-five years old? Joe said before we started here into the future that he'd like to drop in on himself and talk over old times together."

That brought a general laugh. Joe brightened up and thought it would be wonderful. Arthur Granger opened his mouth, as if to begin to talk, when his face winced in pain. Ray felt sure Neal had kicked Arthur under the table. Evidently, he thought, they have had experience with Arthur Granger being foolish before.

"It's a very interesting possibility," Neal said, his eyes twinkling without any sign of his having kicked Granger to quiet him. "But are you sure you want to do that? Suppose the records show that both of you died in—say—1951? Then you would know that when you go back to your own time you will be going to your death."

Very adroit, Ray thought admiringly. Probably Arthur was about to explain to me the impossibility of my finding myself at the age of seventy-five because it would involve a cyclic trap, and Neal has conveyed just the right touch of seeming ignorance.

He decided to pursue the subject.

"It would be worth the risk of finding out such a thing," he said eagerly. "That would be an experience, to actually meet myself as a separate individual… What do *you* say, Joe? Should we look into it?"

"I'm for it," Joe said enthusiastically.

"I suppose I'll have to confess," Val Nelson, who had just come in, spoke up, making a rueful expression. "I thought of that myself and looked up the records without saying anything, so if it turned out something like Neal suggested I could keep still."

"What did you discover?" Ray asked.

"Nothing," Val replied. "I found your birth records. I found evidence of a search for you on suspicion of having caused an explosion that wrecked a building. That's all. No death record, no current evidence of residence anywhere. Of course that doesn't mean you're dead now. It just means that if you're still alive, either one of you, there's nothing in the directories to tell where you live."

A waiter came in and began clearing the table.

There was silence until he had served the dessert and coffee and had departed with the cart of empty dishes. As the door closed behind his back, Arthur Granger turned to Ray with an air of coming down to the business of the meeting.

"We've been making plans for you," he said. "Listen to what we've more or less worked out. Certain ordinary people are allowed in the Vargian buildings—plumbers, janitors, electricians, deliverymen. You will want to explore the area you are suspicious of. We've done that ourselves, so have the experience to keep you out of trouble. You may find some clue we've missed in our searches for Nelva. If you want to do that we can get you a job tomorrow that will give you duties carrying you all over any Vargian district you want to look into first."

"That sounds O.K.," Ray said thoughtfully. He turned to Joe. "I'd like to do this alone—and you stay out of it for now. Stay at the hotel or see the sights with Val. Then if I get caught there'll still be you to come in and pull me out of it."

"Nothing doing," Joe objected. "You can't leave me on the bench. If there's any excitement I intend to be in on it. And I see through your little scheme. It would make you look silly if I happened to rescue Nelva instead of you."

"Natch," Ray grinned. "So keep out of it. Be ready to saddle your trusty steed and ride to the rescue. Pick up a few phone numbers just in case I don't bring the girl friend back with me."

"No," Joe said, pouting, but Ray knew he would.

CHAPTER ELEVEN

RAY BRADLEY'S PULSE quickened with suppressed excitement as he entered the building. All the work of the past three days as a wiring inspector had been directed for this moment. Now he was actually entering the same space that, in 1950, had been occupied by the building housing his office where he had called into the future through a telephone and received a reply.

He glanced at his reflection in the glossy wall surface and smiled grimly. They had disguised him finally—to look like the man whose place he was taking as a wiring inspector. It was all very convincing. He had even had brief doubts and seriously considered the possibility of his being wrong about Val Nelson and the others; but there was too big a backlog of evidence.

So he knew that at least one of the Vargians standing idly in the lobby of the building recognized him and would report ahead that he was now in the building.

He was glad he knew it. It was saving him the nervous anxiety of fearing he would be discovered, and arrested or killed or tortured.

His impulse was to go straight to the rooms on the third floor in the same position as his old office. He resisted it. The Custodians would wonder why he hadn't been careful and might suspect he had outguessed them.

He presented his credentials to the Vargian in charge of the elevator bank and withstood his close and suspicious scrutiny with complete calm.

"Just a minute, please," the Vargian said.

Ray watched him go to a phone at the end of the hall. He watched the Vargian's lips and interpreted the word, "Phony," by reading his lips. When he hung up and came back his lips were smiling but his two eyes were puzzled.

"Everything's O.K.," he said. He took out a key ring and slipped off a key. "This is the master key. Any office that's locked will open to it. It's also your badge of authority. In case of trouble refer whoever it is to the manager of the building or myself."

"Thanks," Ray said. "There shouldn't be any trouble though, should there?" His eyes were innocent as they mocked the elevator captain. He restrained a chuckle at the look of grudging admiration in the Vargian's eyes.

Glancing at his watch he saw it was ten o'clock. He wanted to time things so he would reach the offices that were his goal during the noon hour.

As he paused at the first office door on the second floor he heard girlish tittering inside. When he opened the door it had already stopped. There were six Vargian girls, stenographers, in their early twenties. He had learned that a Vargian aged during the first 20 years at about the same rate as any other person, but didn't begin to show middle age until they were close to a hundred, so these girls were no older than they looked.

They watched him as he prowled around, examining light fixtures, wall outlets, the strange electric fans with no moving parts, and desk lamps. Their eyes smoldered at him. He wondered what would happen if he tried to date one. They certainly invited him to with their eyes.

At the second office he started to put his hand on the doorknob, then drew it back. The girlish tittering sounded again. It stopped as his hand touched the knob to open the door. When he opened it other Vargian girls were intent on their work, but with eyes that darted up at him interestedly.

He was sure now. That third eye was for extra-temporal vision. They could see a little way into the future—perhaps thirty seconds or even more. In both offices they had seen he was going to enter and had tittered in uninhibited excitement, and had quieted before he came in so that he wouldn't suspect they were interested.

And that woman on the bus looked at the spot where her friend would be several seconds in the future, and smiled in recognition and anticipation.

Two eyes able to see things as they are now. A third eye in the forehead that could see a few seconds into the future. What a host of possibilities *that* opened up. Could the future be changed? Could a Vargian see himself trip on something a few seconds in the future and avoid tripping—and thus change the future? Or was the future as unchangeable as the past?

He decided to try finding out. He stopped at one of the desks and smiled at the Vargian girl working there.

"Mind if I ask you a question?" he asked politely.

The girl turned pale and kept her eyes on her work, refusing to answer. He turned away feeling a slow flush spread over his face. The girl's paleness had been due to controlled, intense anger, the anger one feels toward a person of an inferior race who has stepped out of line in a race-conscious community. For the first time in his life Ray felt the bite of being dealt with as an inferior. He was amazed at his reaction. He felt like killing the girl. He felt that if he had a gun he would like to destroy not only her but everyone in that office who had seen his embarrassment and discomfiture.

It was ten minutes after twelve when he stopped outside the door of the office in the same space as his old one had been.

He wasn't enjoying his task any more. The insult to his lineage still rankled. Though he tried to blot it out of his thoughts, it remained, conjuring up elaborate ways of getting revenge equal to the enormity of the insult.

There was no sound of tittering or anything else from the other side of the door. He tried it. It was locked. He grinned without mirth, realizing that the stage was laid. This was his goal, and the Vargians and the Custodians knew it. He wondered bitterly if the Vargians also knew what he would do—not only during the next few seconds, but the next few days. They might.

He used the master key and opened the door. The office was about the same size as his old one—and no one was there. He closed the door and locked it on the inside, then went over and sat down in a chair at a desk near where his telephone had been.

Now, except for a slight matter of forty-nine years and almost three weeks, he was under the same conditions as when he had first heard Nelva appealing to him to escape from the building.

She wasn't here, of course. He had known she wouldn't be. It wouldn't make sense if the Vargians had her. The only thing that made sense was that they wanted her—for some reason—and were using him as bait, or perhaps as a bloodhound to track her down.

She had said in the dream that they could trace her through him while she was in telepathic contact with him. They might be just beyond the walls in the next room waiting with some device so that if she so much as whispered a thought to him they could pounce on her and trace her to her hiding place.

There were eyes watching his every move—had to be. They would be intensely curious about his every move and expression. He was in the center of a stage, and just beyond view was the unseen audience.

Was Nelva one of that audience, hidden from the rest? Ray hoped so. He hoped she was aware of him—could see him or sense his thoughts.

Things were ceasing to be funny any more. The insult to his race had changed things. The third eye with its ability to see into the future was just enough of an argument for racial superiority to add fuel to his feelings.

And Val Nelson, Neal Smith, Craig Blanning, and old Arthur Granger, secure in their naive belief that they were superior to him—able to deceive him successfully.

He let a contemptuous grimace appear on his face. He thought, "There will be a day of reckoning shortly." The thought gave him satisfaction.

He thought of the Vargians patiently watching him through peepholes in the plaster or secret pinhole television cameras that carried his image to some remote part of the building. What would be the expression on their faces if they learned that he knew this was a stage and he had a vast audience? He was tempted to let them know, and laugh at them.

Then, slowly, another idea rose into consciousness. This was a stage. He was the actor. Why not give them an act? Why not *pretend* he was in brief telepathic contact with Nelva? It would present them with a confusing problem—if they were able to detect genuine telepathic communication and follow its energy pattern back to its source.

They might, of course, realize at once that it was fake; but they might also argue to themselves that he would have no reason for faking it, and so puzzle over a red herring. It would be all the more convincing because of the fact that they would be convinced he was not aware he was being watched.

He closed his eyes and rotated his fingers on his temples to appear to be trying to contact Nelva. He formed her name soundlessly with his lips, slowly, several times. He waited, building up suspense in his hidden audience that he was convinced must be there.

The thought struck him that perhaps Nelva was aware of the ruse he was going to pull and was laughing in merriment. The thought made him involuntarily smile. His mind seized on the smile as a starting cue and carried it on. He dropped his fingers from his temples and assumed a listening attitude with his head, keeping his eyes closed. He made himself excited, entered into the spirit of acting even to the extent of imagining the details of a "message" in his mind.

He jerked his head suddenly in assumed bewilderment, then abruptly opened his eyes, blinking them slowly, then shaking his head violently, as though clearing his thoughts.

Then he got up and went directly to the door and let himself out, hammishly peeking to make sure no one was out in the hall. There he hesitated. Should he rush back to the hotel, or should he continue his tour of inspection? He decided to continue his tour. It would keep the Vargians and Custodians on tenterhooks waiting to learn what Nelva had supposedly said to him, and it would give him time to think up something really good.

No doubt even now the Vargians were wondering why their trap had failed and they hadn't been able to trace Nelva. They were probably calling Val Nelson or Arthur Granger and telling them Nelva had contacted him.

He entered another office and began his inspection of electrical things with a reactionary feeling of supreme contempt for the Vargian girls and men there, but gradually his mind settled down to the problem he was now faced with. He had, in effect, committed himself to a whopper of a lie. It would do no good to try to back down by telling the truth; that he hadn't heard the slightest of telepathic whispers from Nelva.

The Custodians, Val, Neal, Craig, and Arthur, would have to appear to accept such a statement or reveal openly their connection with the Vargians—but there another danger presented itself. If he remained secretive they might try to get information out of him by the use of drugs.

Could he get by with a story that Nelva had told him to go to some meeting place alone, and if he was followed or watched she wouldn't appear? If he could put that one over he and Joe would be out of the clutches of the Custodians and the Vargians—and after all, maybe that was just what Nelva was waiting for.

He wished heartily that he knew more about things in this mixed-up civilization of 1999. He didn't even know what made their electric fans work. And that harmless looking little tube thing that could send paralysis through the muscles and tingling torture was something else he knew nothing about.

More relevant to his problem, just what were the Custodians, really? Were they a genuine organization? Were they known to the Vargians as such, and allowed to continue because to destroy them would create revolution? That was possible.

Or were they what he believed them to be: a puppet of the Vargians.

Was there perhaps a genuine underground movement that the Vargians and the Custodians were fighting against? If there were, that would make a lot of sense. Then Nelva would be a part of this unknown group, maybe one of the leaders, and the Vargians would be using him as the lure to trap her and in that way get to the kingpins of the secret group and wipe it out.

Ray thought that over slowly while he continued his tour of inspection. There was only one flaw that he could see in the theory of another underground movement. It couldn't be anything more than a nuisance menace to the Vargians unless it had something that might become a threat. Some secret weapon, perhaps. But then, if they had it why didn't they use it?

His thoughts reverted to the idea of telling Val and the others that Nelva had contacted him and told him to shake off everybody before she would meet him. It was a plausible message, and foolproof, because he could always come back and say he must have been followed or observed, because she didn't show up.

He glanced at his watch and saw it was after four. He could leave now without creating the suspicion that he was foolishly risking suspicion. He smiled inwardly at the complexity of things. Everyone was lying right and left—except Joe. He'd have to practice his story on Joe in the privacy of their hotel room. With Joe believing it, it would be that much easier to put it across.

CHAPTER TWELVE

BACK IN THE hotel Ray found Joe and Val in the lobby dozing in two chairs by the windows. He woke them up and told them with an air of suppressed excitement that it had happened. Val came to his feet instantly.

"Good," he said. "Let's go up to your room where we can talk."

"Did you ask her if she has a girlfriend for me?" Joe asked the moment they reached the room and the door was closed.

"I was too excited to think of it," Ray said.

"What did she say?" Val Nelson asked impatiently. "How is she? Are the Vargians treating her well?"

Ray looked at Val blankly. He had forgotten that Nelva, according to the story that had been dished out to him, was supposed to be in the hands of the Vargians.

"She didn't say how she was or where she was," he said. "She just told me how we could get together."

"How?" Val asked eagerly.

"She said for me and Joe to get out someplace away from town and be sure that no one knew where we were and she would meet us," Ray said. "She stressed the 'no one,' too, as though she meant even you fellows." A malicious impulse possessed him. He added, naively, "I wonder why?"

"I wonder too," Val Nelson said. "It makes me think—" He stopped abruptly.

"It makes you think what?" Ray asked innocently.

"Never mind," Val said. "Let's go over to headquarters so you can tell her father about it."

"Yes," Joe said. "Mr. Granger will be anxious to know you've contacted Nelva, Ray. Maybe we could take him along with us, huh? She couldn't object to that."

"Say, that's an idea," Val said. "Why don't you?"

"She said no one," Ray said frowning. "I'd like to; but look at it this way. You remember she said before that the Vargians could trace her through the contact she made with my mind. If they can do that they have instruments I know absolutely nothing about. Suppose they had such instruments turned on her father. She would know about that and not meet me."

"That could be," Val said, and Ray noted with satisfaction that he was uneasy.

They left the room. Val hung back and was the last one out. Ray saw him turn toward the far corner of the room and dart a questioning glance at the wallpaper halfway up.

"So they have a spy gadget in our room," he thought. "Am I lucky I decided not to voice any of my suspicions to Joe. They would have heard every word."

They caught a taxi to save time, and were soon in Arthur Granger's underground office. Neal and Craig weren't there. Swiftly Ray repeated what he had told Val and Joe; that Nelva had contacted him briefly by telepathy while in one of the offices on his inspection tour and told him that he and Joe must take a jaunt out of town into the country alone. If anyone came along or knew where they were headed she wouldn't meet them.

Val listened impatiently until Ray had told it. He excused himself then with the promise he would be right back. While he was gone Arthur Granger went into an act on how glad he was that his daughter would soon be with him, and how he had looked forward to this day ever since she had been taken from him so long ago.

When Val returned Neal and Craig were with him. He looked distinctly puzzled.

"This is it," Ray thought grimly. "Either they take my story at face value or they know that I'm on to them and it's no use in their pretending any more."

He started to repeat his story to Neal and Craig.

"Val told us," Neal said almost curtly. Realizing he had been too curt, he softened his tone. "I don't like it," he added with a tone of frankness. "The Vargians might be on to it and capture you."

"It's no more risky than my working as an electrical inspector right in their stronghold," Ray objected.

"Ray's right," Arthur Granger said gravely. "There's no way out of it. We must take the risk and let him and Joe go out and meet her."

That, Ray thought, was as neat a bit of double talk as he had ever heard. His respect for the old man's abilities shot up.

"When is this rendezvous?" Craig Blanning asked.

"She didn't say," Ray answered. "I gathered that the sooner the better, however. Even right now."

He thought, "If Joe and I can only get away scot free from this crowd of liars we won't come back, whatever happens."

"Are you sure she contacted you and you didn't imagine it?" Val asked desperately.

With that question Ray knew Val had talked with the Vargians and been told that they didn't get the slightest trace of a telepathic bearing, and that either there had been none or something new had been added to things.

"Of course I didn't imagine it!" he said indignantly. "What reason would I have for that?"

"That's it," Val said, addressing his remark more to his three fellow Custodians than to Ray. "You would have no reason to."

And that, as Ray had hoped would be the case, was the thing that clinched matters. He would have had no reason for faking a message from Nelva, so far as they could figure. If they could have thought of a reason they would certainly have accepted the evidence of their instruments that no telepathic contact had been made; but any reason for taking it would have had to have been based on the assumption that Ray knew they were lying themselves—and that they just couldn't accept, Ray felt sure.

"Well," Neal Smith said, as though making a decision on a bad bargain, "it's about time for dinner. Suppose we eat, and then you two can go out and keep your rendezvous."

"The rest of you eat," Val spoke up hastily. "I'll go out and rent a car for them so it'll be all ready when they are."

"A good idea," Ray said approvingly.

Val caught a taxi, which took him directly to the building where Ray had spent most of the day supposedly inspecting light fixtures. There was a preoccupied frown on his face as he entered the building and took the elevator to the tenth floor. He was obviously well known to the attendants in the building. He had told the truth when he had said no one was permitted in the areas occupied by the Vargians unless they had known business there.

He strode quickly down the hall on the tenth floor and opened a door without knocking. The room he entered was large, taking up the full length of the building. There were several dozen Vargians here, all busily watching banks of television screens that brought varied scenes to view from all over the city.

He ignored these and walked through the long room to a door at the far end, in the same wall as that through which he had entered. This time he knocked. A voice was telling him to come in even as he knocked—but he was used to the Vargian ability to see a little way into the future. He opened the door and entered a room where half a dozen Vargians sat around a table in some sort of conference.

These were Vargians such as Ray and Joe hadn't seen. They were old men, stoop shouldered and with gray hair. Their skins were wrinkled. Their two eyes like normal people's were faded.

But in the forehead of each of them the third eye was startlingly different than in those Ray and Joe had seen. In each of them that third eye was brightly alive with strange forces that swirled and danced.

Val paused after he closed the door. He swallowed loudly several times. He always felt helpless and uncomfortable in the presence of these Vargians that sat here, quietly, day after day, and guided the destinies of both Vargians and men.

They looked at him, their faces expressionless. They were waiting for him to speak.

Briefly he told them what had happened. They listened until he stopped talking. Then one of them came to life, smiling slowly, mirthlessly.

"It seems," he said, "that Ray Bradley has known all along that you were lying to him. It seems he has a full and accurate estimation of everything, and has been playing the game with your cards, Val Nelson."

"I don't think so," Val said, paling. "He hasn't the ability to do that without our catching on. And you know how elaborately we've kept him under observation. We've worked together on that, so that even on the street his faintest whispered word could be overheard and reported. Not by one word, even to Joe Ashford in private, has he even indirectly hinted at being suspicious of us."

"That's true," another of the Vargians admitted. "But it is also true beyond question that Nelva didn't contact him. He made it up."

"Oh well," the Vargian at the head of the table said tiredly, as though a discussion had been going on before Val Nelson arrived. "The fact remains that he might possibly get in contact with Nelva on this projected outing—and if he does it will be over in an instant. If he doesn't, he can't escape. We have guards at the place where his time machine will arrive in another ten days. We had them there before, when they arrived."

"I wish I knew more of what's behind all this," Val said in a voice that was half pleading, half fearful.

Six triplets of eyes rested on him frigidly. He swallowed again noisily and backed toward the door.

"You will refrain from being curious, Mr. Nelson," a stern voice spoke. "You will live just so long as you serve us well and without question. That goes for the others of you. I will say only this. Ray Bradley and Joe Ashford must meet Nelva, and under conditions where we can do what we have in mind to do—or neither you nor we will live to correct our errors."

"But don't you see?" Val became bolder. "I *want* to understand. I *want* to be able to serve you better—by understanding what it's all about so I can act intelligently instead of blindly. I understand why you Vargians came and occupied the United States. It was to save us from another war—to save civilization. I know a lot. Enough for me to be entirely and wholeheartedly behind you; but I feel I should understand this threat that hangs around the mysterious Nelva and these two clods from the dark ages of 1950."

"And if you knew," the Vargian at the head of the table said, "you would try to use your own judgment, and probably make mistakes. I will say just this. It will enable you to understand better the problem confronting us. Nelva has been able to hide from us in *time,* rather than space. We can only get to her if Ray gets to her. Only she among all twentieth century peoples has solved a little riddle of time that enabled her to do so. In solving that riddle she also found the way to, in all practical effects, destroy us. Does that answer your question sufficiently?"

"I hope so," Val said doubtfully. "I don't understand, but maybe I will after thinking about it. Thank you, sires."

He backed out of the room respectfully.

CHAPTER THIRTEEN

THE HIGHWAY was a four laned ribbon along which blurred shapes streaked at unbelievable speeds. Painted into the lanes every half mile or so were numbers to serve as continual reminders to motorists to maintain their speed or get out of the lane. There was no oncoming traffic. All four lanes went in the same direction.

Joe kept the car in the extreme right hand lane, which alone had no painted numbers. The one next to it said one hundred, and next to that, one fifty. The left hand lane had a minimum speed of two hundred. Joe was creeping at eighty-five in the low speed lane.

Ray sat beside him in the front seat, watching him with secret amusement. Most of the cars that whizzed by in the hundred mile lane were doing a hundred and forty. An occasional car came along in the two hundred mile lane, appearing for a second or two behind, staying in sight ahead for another three seconds.

A car crept up behind them and honked impatiently. Joe looked bewilderedly at the ditch, then grinned nervously at Ray and held his ground. With an insulting blast the other car darted around him. Almost immediately after it pulled into the hundred mile lane and dwindled into the distance.

"How far we going?" Joe asked, relaxing a little.

The question sobered Ray. "I don't know yet," he answered, and he didn't. There were things to do yet that he couldn't explain to Joe. The first was to get rid of the car, their clothes, and everything else, right down to the skin, and replace everything with things that could not possibly contain secret devices by which the Vargians and Custodians could keep track of them. If he explained that to Joe now, there would be a strong chance of the Vargians picking them up before they could disappear.

The car must go first, but in a way that wouldn't arouse suspicion. A wreck. Or was a wreck necessary? Engine trouble might work just as well.

"Let's stop at the next roadside joint," he suggested. "I could do with some refreshments."

"Me too," Joe grunted, swerving off the highway onto a driveway leading into the parking lot of a rather large country cocktail bar and restaurant. He drove into a parking place.

When they got out of the car Ray saw that Joe had taken the keys and dropped them into his suit coat pocket.

Another car had driven in just behind them. Three men and three girls were converging with them toward the ornate entrance to the place.

As they reached the doors Ray stumbled against Joe, picking the keys out of his pocket, jouncing Joe against one of the men. There were profuse apologies, Ray, slipping the keys in his pocket, accepted full blame for everything. One of the men insisted it was his fault, as he thought he must have tripped Ray, since he was right behind him.

Inside, Ray and Joe went to the bar. The three men and their girl friends took a table ten feet away. Ray waited until the bartender had brought their drinks.

"Be back in a minute, Joe," he said casually. "Keep my place for me."

"Not if I can coax a girl away from that party we bumped into coming in," Joe said happily.

Ray laughed and sipped his drink before leaving. As he made his way toward the men's room one of the three men in the party detached himself and followed him. He fell into step beside Ray.

"Listen, friend," he said softly. "Let's step outside a minute. I want to make a deal with you."

"What is it?" Ray asked in a voice that wouldn't carry. "Why not here? There's lots of noise."

The stranger looked around warily.

"You're right," he mumbled. "Listen. How would you like to rent me your car for the rest of the night? I'll give you a hundred bucks, and have it back in town at any garage you say by nine o'clock tomorrow morning."

Ray concealed a look of exultation. He looked knowingly at the man.

"Too crowded with six of you, huh?" he grinned.

"Exactly," the man said. "Tell you what—I'll make it a hundred and fifty. Then if we scratch a fender it'll be taken care of ahead of time, and if we don't you're that much ahead."

"You're on," Ray agreed, reaching into his pocket and getting the keys. "But there's one condition attached to it."

"What's that?" the stranger asked doubtfully.

"Get your girlfriend and scram with it right away," Ray said.

"Fair enough," the man said, exchanging three fifty dollar bills for the keys.

Ray returned to the bar feeling very self satisfied.

The car couldn't have been disposed of more satisfactorily if it had been planned that way. In the morning it would be returned to the city by someone who wouldn't be able to tell a thing out of the way.

"What's the matter with you?" Joe asked tolerantly. "You look like the cat that swallowed the canary. You're actually licking your chops."

Ray watched the stranger and his girlfriend move toward the entrance through the backbar mirror without answering. Joe looked at him, then let his eyes wander over the huge interior of the place, with its tables, dance floor, bar, and orchestra.

"All we need is a girlfriend," Joe grumbled. "All this is wasted without one. No kiddin'."

"Maybe that can be fixed," Ray said slyly. He sipped his cocktail while his eyes studied the activity around them. They settled finally on two young ladies sitting in a booth. They were alone, and Ray remembered now that they had been alone over there when he and Joe came in.

He nudged Joe, who looked at him, following the direction of his gaze until he discovered the two girls.

"They look good from here," Joe said. "But most of them do from this distance."

The two girls were looking at them.

"Let's go over," Joe said, rising and starting over, Ray followed, regretting the impulse that had prompted him to start this. It would serve a purpose though. It would kill time, and might conceivably lead to a ride to the next city.

As they approached the booth Ray studied the two girls. One of them seemed to appeal to him in some way. She was dark haired, her face extremely white and smooth, but with an expression of strain lurking on it. Her eyes were large and round—which added to the air of tenseness. Her lips smiled anxiously as he paused with Joe in front of the table.

"May we join you?" Joe asked politely.

"Please do," Ray heard the other girl say. He sat down beside the dark haired girl, his eyes still studying her.

"I'm Joe," Ray heard Joe say. "And this is my pal, Ray."

"I'm Nancy," Ray heard the other girl say. "And this is my friend, Nelva."

"Nelva?" Joe exploded. But Ray was looking deep into her large blue eyes and realizing that he had instinctively known it was her. More, he had known she would be here—but how he knew was something he couldn't understand.

His eyes broke with hers and turned to roam over the place warily.

"We'll leave quickly," he heard Nelva murmur in his ear. Her voice thrilled him. He nodded.

"Let's go right now," he said suddenly, gruffly. "Suddenly this place seems full of danger."

"It is," Nelva said. She laid a hand on his arm. Her fingers bit into his flesh.

Pins and needles pricked every cell of his body for three terrible seconds. It ended abruptly. His vision cleared. The room seemed no different than it had been. There were people, music, and chatter. But suddenly Ray knew it was not the same. That feeling had been the same one he and Joe had experienced in time travel. The faces about them were different. He turned to Nelva.

"Which way did we travel?" he asked. "Into the future?"

"No, Ray," Nelva said. "We've gone back to the day you arrived here in 1999. This is May nineteenth, nineteen ninety-nine."

Ray heard Joe whistle softly in amazement. His head was spinning with bewilderment.

"But it can't be," he heard himself saying. "I've already worked out the theory of timelines that shows such a thing to be impossible. Anyway, where's your time travel machine? We were just sitting in this booth and presto, we are in a different time."

"Let's leave," Nelva urged gently. "We have lots to do, and lots to talk about—but we can't do it here."

"Wait," Ray demanded. "Let me get this one thing clear in my mind. We're here—and we, Joe and I, are also back in town—" He glanced at his watch. "Just about ready to go to bed after having met Val Nelson and the others."

"That's right," Nelva agreed.

"Then," Ray hesitated, "for the next few days we can accomplish things while the other of me is going through everything I remember doing?"

"Yes," Nelva answered.

"But it isn't possible," Ray said doggedly. "It would mean dualism of position for every atom of my body, and most of them are the same atoms. It means a time-trap, in which I go forward in time to suddenly jump back to the start again, over and over again."

"Nothing of the sort," Nelva said. "Tomorrow you will get the whole picture. We're out of danger for the present. But we have work to do tomorrow, so let's leave now."

CHAPTER FOURTEEN

IT WAS one of those rambling one-story countryside residences of the type designed by an architect who knows how to fit structure to living gracefully. Outside each window was a delightful world of plants and birds and squirrels, all so unconcerned about what went on inside that they carried their love making and fighting right up to the sills of the full-length windows.

Ray awakened to all this from the most restful sleep he had had in a long time. He showered in a dream of glistening glass and chrome, dressed in clothes that had been laid out for him while he slept, and which were all new and never worn.

In a kitchen designed for modern living he fell in love with Nelva instantly, in her red checkered housedress. She looked up from frying ranch style eggs and flashed him a smile. Joe and Nancy were in the breakfast nook in the midst of their breakfast already.

Ray stood just inside the doorway looking at all this. His eyes returned to Nelva. He guessed that it must have been she who laid out his clothes while he slept, she who must have bought them.

"Well, come on in and get comfortable," Joe ordered jovially. "Don't stand there gawking."

"There's plenty to gawk at," Ray said, catching Nelva's eye. He walked across the room purposefully and took Nelva's face between his hands and kissed her on the lips while she protested mildly, smiling with her lips and her blue eyes.

Those blue eyes followed him tenderly as he went over to the nook and sat down opposite Joe and Nancy. He thought: it's a very rare thing for a man to find a girl with the same abilities and interests.

It was clumsy to put it that way, but the clumsy words covered everything. He let Joe and Nancy do the talking while he ate, with Nelva sitting beside him, also eating. He finished. Nancy got up and poured more coffee for them. Cigarettes appeared from somewhere—Joe had them and gave him one.

"Now then, dream girl," Ray said, smiling at Nelva. "Tell me. You know what I want to know. Everything. Who are you, when and where do you originally come from, how did you accomplish the impossible in time travel—and without any gadgets that I could see, and why am I necessary in all this, since it's obvious that your knowledge is so far above mine that I can't possibly contribute anything to yours?"

"What would you say if I were a Vargian?" Nelva asked. She watched his face anxiously.

"But you aren't," Ray said. "You're shorter—barely five feet five, while they're over six, and you don't have the extra-temporal eye."

"Then let's put it this way," Nelva said. "What if the Vargians were just plain human beings? Suppose any married couple could have Vargian children if they wanted them?"

"How would it be done?" Ray asked. "That would mean the Vargians are a mutation on the human race, and a controlled mutation that could be repeated at will. Is it inheritable, or does every Vargian child have to undergo the operation or whatever it is?"

"You're getting close," Nelva said. "A Vargian is just an ordinary human being at birth, though of a strain different than the modern ones."

"Then how do they get that third eye?" Ray asked.

"At birth they're placed under a standardized machine that rests on their forehead," Nelva said. "It's a variation of the time solenoid. It draws some of the cells of the skin and bone of their foreheads as far as thirty seconds into the future. Actually it makes a time bridge of matter.

"You see, all matter is time broad. The instantaneous present that we picture as moving forward into the future from the past is an abstraction. In actuality it is a crest whose peak is the now that we conceive as having no actual extent in time. From that peak it drops off into the past a split second ago, and into the future a split second from now.

"I'll show you the mathematics of it later on when we have the time, but you can guess at it now when I tell you that two particles near enough to each other to act on one another act like two waves. Your scientists before 1950 got a glimpse of that, vaguely. What they couldn't have guessed, of course, is that one particle can be permanently pulled out of phase with another, either into the past or the future, just enough so that it still acts on the other, but also is acted on more by other particles still farther into the future.

"You can picture it three dimensionally by an alternating current in a wire. The pressure wave of one cycle goes forward along the wire at the speed of light. It's analogous to the reality of the present, traveling forward into the future at a constant speed—and that analogy is more basic than you would think at first, because the speed of light and the rate of time are basically connected in the four dimensional continuum.

"So in the extra-temporal eye of the Vargian we have living matter pulled out of phase with the rest of reality and susceptible to reality as it will be from the present to about thirty seconds into the future. It's a permanent complex, and gets its nourishment from the bloodstream just as easily as it would otherwise, pulling new matter forward in time with it, shoving it back into the general wave crest again."

"I think I can see that, a little," Ray said slowly. "It answers one question by bringing up another, though. I always thought matter was particulate, and moved in space. You make it sound like there's some four dimensionally stationary basic substance we don't know of, and matter and our reality are actually some kind of an energy flow in it."

"That's exactly so," Nelva said eagerly. "All reality is merely an energy flow along a four dimensional stationary reality, like a pulse of current along a wire. The actions of units of matter on one another, the complexes of structure of matter, are merely mutually inductive wave fronts that affect one another, Einstein guessed that. He expressed the hope that eventually the particulate structure of matter could be dispensed with, and the field theory account for everything. He could have accomplished that by considering the basic particles of matter as being what they really are—wave packets travelling at the speed of light at right angles to all space directions."

"At the speed of light?" Ray echoed.

"In a way that's inaccurate," Nelva said. "What I meant was, at a constant speed—like the speed of light is constant. Actually it isn't a speed at all, in the sense that it's a distance covered."

"That's what I thought," Ray said. "I considered it more like a stationary change, like the increase in pressure in a tire, or, in an actual case, the aging of an individual over the years."

"That's probably the only way we can approach an understanding of it," Nelva went on. "Anyway, to get back to the Vargian eye, it's not a normal body organ at all, but an artificial one. It makes a lens of sorts that focuses on the cortex of the brain and builds up a visual center. Events in the near future are enough out of phase with current reality wave so they don't have much effect on the present; but in the extra-temporal lens they work down by induction so that the energy patterns that strike the brain cells are enough in phase to produce an effect."

"Then if the Vargian child were not submitted to this change it would be just an ordinary human?" Joe put in.

"That's right," Nelva admitted. "So in that sense I'm a Vargian. I belong to the same race."

"But you're so much shorter," Joe said. "Vargian women are over six feet tall."

"That height is a side effect of the third eye," Nelva explained. "It changes around some of the departments of the brain and produces the extra growth."

"Where did the Vargians come from?" Ray asked.

"I've been building up to that," Nelva said. "I've been trying to build up a picture of reality as a sort of pressure wave in an underlying reality, traveling along at a constant speed called time. A sharp wave like a sound wave traveling through water. In addition there are broader waves, like the large waves of the ocean that beat against a shore. It's complicated, but it's there. The Vargians come from another of these broad waves. They aren't from your past or future, as you might think. They are a different wave traveling the same path. Their reality is out of phase with this one.

"They discovered time travel, and accidentally stumbled onto your parallel reality. Realizing you would soon discover time travel yourselves, they decided to forestall that—prevent it."

"Wait a minute," Joe said. "Let's get back to the subject of you being a Vargian. Why aren't you like the others then?"

"In Varga the third eye is not given to everyone," Nelva explained. "Only to certain classes. Varga is a matriarchy, and, well, Nancy and I were not the eldest daughters, so we were not given the third eye so we could never assume the throne."

"Then you're from the royal family?" Joe asked, looking from Nancy to Nelva in awe.

"We're younger sisters of the queen," Nancy answered. "You've met her, I think. Her picture is everywhere."

"We've met her picture," Joe said grimly. "Personally I hope we never meet her in person. She looks like she could smile at you and cut your throat at the same time."

"She's like that," Nelva said. "It was she who conceived the scheme of taking over the control of your race. It was foolproof, except that I, in the progress of my education, stumbled onto something about time travel that hadn't been known before."

"This skipping back and living two parts of your life at once?" Ray asked.

"That's part of it," Nelva admitted. "The main part of it is that I can create what you call a time trap and what I call an eddy circuit in the time stream, and tie them up in it, freeing the human race in this wave forever from the other."

"So that's what they fear," Ray said softly. "I had an idea it was something like that." He frowned at the table surface for a few seconds. "But what part do I play in it? What I mean is…I've gathered the impression that in some way I'm vital to the whole thing. I find now that my knowledge is elementary compared to yours on the subject of time travel. I can't add to your knowledge. I'm certainly not indispensable physically."

"I can't tell you the part you play—yet," Nelva said. "You'll know when it's all over—and that will be soon. I promise."

"And then you go back to your wave of reality and I don't see you any more?" Ray asked, watching her closely.

"That depends," she said, but there was a look in her eyes that seemed to say, "—on you."

There was a lapse in the conversation. A bright sun sent its cheery rays into the kitchen, making everything more vivid. The silence was broken by Joe snorting.

"I just thought of something," he said. "If we go back and sit in that booth in the roadhouse at the time we were sitting there, we will in effect have lived almost a week in the twinkling of an eye. Incidentally, we disappeared from there without paying our bill."

"How *did* we get back?" Ray asked. "You wrapped your fingers around my arm, Nelva, and then we came back in time."

"That's something the Varg Thrott would like to learn," Nelva answered. "My grasping your arm had nothing to do with it. I did that merely to steady you. The mechanism—it's something special that I've been working on a long time. It's as much of an improvement over your time travel machine that you came to 1999 in as—as the modern radio is over the first one ever built." She was getting up from the table as she said, "We could sit here all day and talk. There's too much to do. I can explain things as we go along much better. Today we must go into the city and follow you around in your timeline as it starts from having breakfast with Val Nelson."

"What?" Ray and Joe exclaimed in unison.

CHAPTER FIFTEEN

"THIS IS GOING to seem strange, spooky, to you," Nelva said as they climbed out of her car, parked across the street from the cafeteria. "Remember what I told you. When you press hard on the control hidden in your pocket it will bring you into quarter phase with the time front that is real to you as you were. With your finger off the control button you're practically out of phase—and therefore relatively non-existent to it."

It was definitely spooky, Ray and Joe studied the shadowy world about them with wide-eyed wonder. A car was headed directly toward them. They jumped out of its path instinctively—and turned to see the car pass right through Nelva and Nancy without seeming to affect them in any way. The girls smiled at their alarmed expressions.

"It's just like it was all three-dimensional images of light instead of solid substance," Joe marveled.

"That's what it actually is to us as we are now," Nelva said. "Solidity is relative. We can walk through a solid object just as if it were the beam of a flashlight."

"Then why don't we sink into the ground?" Ray asked.

"You do, a little," Nelva smiled. Ray and Joe looked down. Sure enough, the shadowy surface of the pavement cut into their feet half an inch above the soles. Nelva explained. "We're just a wee shade in phase with ordinary reality, and that amount of juxtaposition is enough to give us traction and maintain our position. There you are," she added, pointing toward the plate glass front of the cafeteria.

Joe and Ray had already seen what she was pointing to. They were inside, with Val Nelson. Ray was in the act of placing one of the three capsules in his mouth. Joe was looking at him, laughing.

"That gives me an uncanny feeling," Joe murmured. "I can remember that. It's like seeing a movie of something I was in."

They moved through the door, feeling its slight drag as it passed through them. Some people came through the door behind them and pushed through them without being aware of it.

"Is this the explanation of the spirit world?" Ray asked, watching the backs of those who had just gone through them.

"I don't know," Nelva said. "This is what might be called *i*-time, using the conventions of mathematics. A time stream separated from the regular one by a little 'distance' in what could be considered the fifth-dimension. It's something the Vargian rulers don't know about. If they did they could find me."

They stood and watched the progress of the breakfast. When it was over they followed themselves and Val Nelson as they left the cafeteria.

Ray remembered that they had made a tour of the city. He turned to Nelva.

"What's the reason for our following ourselves around like this?" he asked. "There must be a reason."

"There is," Nelva said. "Remember—as you lived this other period—that at night you couldn't sleep, and you took a walk during which you arrived at certain conclusions about Val and Neal and the other Custodians?"

"Yes," Ray said doubtfully.

"Well," Nelva said. "This may sound strange to you, but you came to those conclusions largely because of this trip we are taking with you. Wait and see if it isn't true."

"But how could that be?" Ray asked incredulously. "That's already happened and we can't change it. Why, right now we could turn and walk away from all this, and it would go on without the slightest change."

"Could you?" Nelva asked, smiling. "Aren't you assuming that the 'past' is fixed while the 'present' is changeable? Actually none of it is changeable, past or future or present. In your memory you went through all that over there in the shadow world days ago—but actually at that same time you were over here doing what you're doing right now. They both happened and are happening at the same time."

"But that's absurd," Ray exclaimed heatedly. "Then I was 'over' there, aware only of what went on around me there."

"So the difference is in the location of your seeming awareness," Nelva said. "All right, I'll show you something."

She fumbled in the bag she was carrying and brought out a small pillbox. She took out a capsule and handed it to Ray.

"Swallow this," she ordered. After he had obeyed her she went on. "That's a hypnotic of a certain type that will make your mind more receptive of suggestion. It acts quickly."

"I don't feel anything," Ray said.

"You won't," Nelva said. "It's a very dangerous drug. It practically wrecked the economy of the United States at one time. You can slip that powder in a cup of coffee and in a few minutes a man will sign over his entire fortune to you without an argument. Close your eyes."

Ray did so instantly.

"Now," Nelva said. "It is the day after you arrived in the future. You are with Val and Joe. Are you?"

Ray nodded.

"O.K.," Nelva said. "Look around behind you."

The shadow Ray Bradley looked around idly in their direction.

"Now you are with me," Nelva said. "Open your eyes."

Ray opened his eyes. He looked over at his shadow form queerly.

"For an instant," he said. "I would swear I was right back in that second day."

"You were," Joe said. "Nelva asked you to look around and your shadow head did."

"It did?" Ray exclaimed. "I thought I moved my head here."

"No," Joe said. "I looked both places to make sure."

"Now do you understand?" Nelva said. "With your conscious mind you affected events over there in the shadow world—events that you considered unchangeable. They *are* unchangeable. If you have a clear enough memory you will remember changing your head around over there—perhaps wondering what made you look over this way."

"No," Ray said doubtfully. "I can't remember, but you must be right. I see what you mean though. But what about consciousness? I am certainly not aware over there now…"

"But you are," Nelva said. "What is consciousness? Thought goes on in your mind outside of your current range of consciousness all the time. Subconscious thought, it's called. Inspiration, perhaps. It pushes through from one level to another, from the past as memory, from the future as inspiration or premonition or foresight or prophecy."

"Then I am going to talk to myself tonight," Ray said. "I'm convinced. I can see it now."

"That's right," Nelva said. "Although you can be conscious only of the three dimensional being, you are really a multi-dimensional being through which consciousness flows. If you could see yourself as a whole you would see the continuity of structure connecting your shadow body and your present one, and really understand they are just two cross sections of the one person—slightly bent back to run parallel for a short period."

One of the innumerable three-dimensional pictures of the Vargian queen was looking down at them at the moment.

"What's your sister, the queen's, name?" Joe asked. "Queen Vargia," Nelva said. "That's custom. It's also custom for the second born girl to be named Nelva, and the third, Nancy, in the royal family."

"I just thought of something," Joe said. "Why can't we go ahead, into the future this way and see how things are going to turn out—or have you done that already?" He looked slyly at Nelva.

"It might be possible," Nelva said. "Nancy and I tried it—without success. We couldn't find ourselves. It isn't even possible right now to make you in your shadow body look and see you as you are here, because you would have to penetrate the barrier of that other consciousness level. I have heard, though, of so-called adepts of past ages, who could see their future ahead of them clearly right up to the moment of death. Christ himself was supposed to be able to see his crucifixion, and more than once told his disciples what they were going to do before they did it."

"Then maybe this *is* the spirit realm here in the world we're in now," Ray said.

"I don't know," Nelva said. "It may be. The five-dimensional solenoid is my own discovery. It's what enables us to be here in the state of existence we're in. It's an elaboration of the four-dimensional one you discovered by yourself, Ray. I'm just beginning to understand its full potentialities. It could be that I'm the originator of it, and future generations are using it now, and have used it in all past ages. Time travel sort of mixes things up. It can make the causes of things in the past come from the future, and make things we see happening long ago have their origin in something in a future age."

As they talked they followed their shadow forms around the city, their eyes taking in everything from a different angle. Ray was seeing the things that made him suspicious of Val Nelson. He was seeing them, and realizing that in his present consciousness he was in reality a part of his own subconscious, so far as his conscious level of that previous period was concerned. He commented on this.

"Yes," Nelva said. "Probably you've read of hypnotists taking a person back to their childhood and the remarkable results. It's really the same thing. You as you were at six or five or even newborn, still exist in the time stream at that date. It's all one connected multi-dimensional object."

"I'm trying to understand it all," Ray said. "It must be the complete basic picture of everything. Your plan—I know it's probably too deep for me to understand yet, but it must depend on this i-time stream we're in."

"It does," Nelva said, her face serious. "I wish I could tell you all of it, but you'll see in the end why I couldn't."

She placed her hand on his arm and looked into his eyes.

"I hope you'll always have trust in me," she added. "There may be a time shortly when you might find that hard to do."

"How can I help trusting you when you are so beautiful," Ray smiled. But there was a thoughtful look on his face as he turned away.

The day wore on and came to a close. The shadow Ray, Joe, and Val returned to the hotel rooms. When they entered the four followed them into the room.

Nelva looked around curiously, finally went over and studied the space behind the dresser.

"Come over here, Ray," she said.

Ray looked where she pointed. There was a small box behind the dresser.

"That's a snooper," Nelva said. "Warn yourself not to say anything out of the way in this room. Just close your eyes and visualize yourself as you were—are in the other time-line, and will the information down the line. It'll get there—unvoiced."

"Your own guardian angel," Joe said.

"No kidding," Ray answered seriously. "So much of all this explains so much of the mysteries of the world."

"Perhaps more so than you suspect even yet," Nancy spoke up.

"Atta girl, Nancy," Joe Ashford said. "I'll bet you know a lot more than you let on. You seem to let Nelva do all the intellectual spouting, but I'll bet if you wanted to you could show her a thing or two."

"Don't overestimate me, Joe," Nancy said, laughingly. "But you seem the quiet type, too. Are you sure that back there on the other 'side' you didn't suspect the Custodians too?"

"Had them pegged right from the start," Joe said blandly. The twinkle in his eye was too much. All four of them laughed. "There's only one thing that puzzles me," Joe finally managed to say—but that brought further laughter.

"What's the one thing you don't understand?" Ray asked.

"How can we talk to one another and laugh and everything here in the hotel room without it being heard by us in the other world?"

"That's easily explained," Ray said self-consciously. Nelva and Nancy smiled. "Matter is 'physical' only toward other matter in phase with it. We're out of phase with the other side, and so is the atmosphere we breathe. If there were nothing but the other atmosphere we wouldn't get enough oxygen. When we talk we affect only the atmospheric molecules in phase with us. Isn't that right, Nelva?"

"Perfectly," she agreed. "There is a small carry-over, though. If the room were perfectly quiet and you, over there, were listening for it, you could hear what is said."

"There we go again," Joe said. "Spirit voices."

"Is that how you spoke to me back in 1950, Nelva?" Ray asked. "I thought it was telepathy across time, and that you were talking to me from 1999 A.D." He saw by the expression on her face that he had found the answer. "There goes a romantic dream," he said with pretended disgust. "Here I thought we were two souls attuned, and I find you just talked to me like you could have to anyone else."

"There, there, sonny," Joe soothed. "She loves you anyway—don't you, Nelva?"

"That's not fair," Nelva said, turning an obvious pink.

CHAPTER SIXTEEN

"AFTER BREAKFAST you're going to meet some of my friends," Nelva said. It was nearly noon of the next day. All four of them had stuck with Ray on the "other side" during his night of restlessness and deep thought.

"I've been wondering about that," Joe Ashford said through a mouthful of toast and marmalade.

"There's quite a colony of us," Nelva spoke up. "A few of us second-born Vargians, and several Americans—most of them in their seventies."

"People full grown before the Vargians took over the country?" Ray suggested.

"That's right," Nelva said, pouring the coffee. "One of the first things the Vargians did was change the textbooks so as to indoctrinate the younger generations. There are very few Americans under fifty that don't firmly believe Vargian rule is necessary for world peace and prosperity."

"You ought to read some of the grade school textbooks," Nancy cut in. "But maybe you'd better not. You might believe them and turn against us. It *is* true that the presence of the Vargians with their weapons so infinitely superior to anything the rest of the world can produce has prevented a war—so far."

"How far from the future did the Vargians come?" Ray asked. "A million years?"

"They came from the past," Nelva said. She smiled mischievously. "By the most accurate of measurements I was born in 357224 B.C.. Right here in America, too; though at that time America was much different."

"I imagine it was," Joe said. "What was it like then?"

"In those days," Nelva said. "The middle west was ocean. The present Rocky Mountains were the eastern coast of a vast continent covering much of what is now the Pacific.

"It's strange how land masses change so much, while here and there small areas remain unchanged over millions of years. From the Olympic mountains in the state of Washington, down through a good part of Oregon and northern California the land hasn't changed hardly at all. The mountain peaks Rainier and Shasta probably have snow near their peaks that first fell over a million years ago. At one time those two mountains could be seen far out at sea from the east. To the west of them stretched the continent legend knows as Mu or Lemuria, generally believed to be the cradle of mankind, though the origin of mankind was as mysterious to us in those days as it is now."

"Mmm-*mh!*" Joe exclaimed. "How about the Cro-Magnons and other ancient races said to live just a few thousand years ago?"

"Probably degenerates," Nelva said. "Even today if civilization were to end in some cataclysm and only a few isolated bands were to survive, the big hairy brutes with the most cunning would kill off the more civilized males and take over. In a dozen generations you'd have another race of 'prehistoric men' whose bones would make nice studies in the rise of man from the ape or sub-man."

Joe nodded his head in thoughtful agreement.

"That's probably so," he said. "Back in my own time I liked to attend wrestling matches, and if you go to them often enough you eventually see specimens that would fit the classification all right. You can even see them every day on the street. It would be survival of the fittest, with the fittest being the toughest rather than the smartest, the ones with no compunctions rather than those with humanitarian instincts."

"That's right," Nelva agreed. "Anyway, in 357224 B.C., or 1469 A.V.—meaning 'Ante Vargot,' explorers in time travel ships were going into the future. From all parts of Varmour they were searching forward. Many of them met with disaster—which was easy. They did like you two did. They built stationary ships designed purely for time travel. If their base ground sunk a few hundred feet before they slipped back into the time-stream again they found themselves falling and cracking up—or floating on the Pacific. Or even underground.

"Here and there they found safe spots for highways into the future. Spots like the caverns in Mt. Shasta and Mt. Rainier and Mt. Olympus on the Olympic Peninsula. The Mt. Shasta one was the first, and from it they explored in your early twentieth century and found the others. All through the world you can find the time-tracks of their travels, mysterious fields of warpage."

"Yes, we know," Ray said quietly. "When we arrived here in 1999 and sent our ship back to 1950 we saw the warpage of space it caused, and recognized its similarity to such spots as the one near Santa Cruz in California and Gold Hill in Oregon."

"There are many more," Nelva said. "There's lots of them in the upper atmosphere, I think it was in 1956 that a blimp mapped one a couple of thousand feet in the air in Mendocino County, California. There are lots of them in that area, and out over the Pacific are several hundred in the air. They aren't noticeable to the pilot of a plane because he's through one so quickly and thinks its effect on the ship is atmospheric."

"Just what causes one?" Joe asked. "I suppose," he gave Ray a tolerant smile, "Ray has it all figured out; but I haven't."

"Let's see if Ray has," Nelva smiled. "What do you think, Ray?"

"It's the principle of the little man who wasn't there," Ray answered. "Matter is essentially basic matter particles such as electrons, and nuclei, rushing here and there. The matter results in fields, but there's a time lapse between the origin of the field at the particles and its distribution through surrounding space. With time travel the matter particles are moving forward in time as well as in all directions in space. So it leaves its field in space like the wake of a boat through water. And like with the boat, the wake-field of matter in time travel is different in some ways than it would be for the same matter drifting with the normal time stream.

"You can walk right through it because there isn't any matter there to stop you. It's the little man who, at every instant, has just left. The fields are still here, however, and they refract light, offer resistance to movement, and so on."

"That's right," Nancy said, pretending to be crestfallen.

"But what I want to know," Ray said, "is, why did the Vargians come forward in time and live? Why didn't they stay in their own time?"

"There were several factors involved," Nelva said. "First, it was the natural impulse to expand—the same motive that made the English expand all over the world and exploit and develop. Second, they early discovered that in a few centuries Varmour was destined to sink and become the bed of the modern Pacific Ocean. Third, they discovered twentieth century civilization at its peak in America, and so naturally chose this era and civilization as being the only one in the future capable of supporting them in the manner to which they were accustomed."

"I see," Ray said slowly. "They simply moved in, with as little disturbance as they could of the status quo."

"Well, I want to know something myself," Joe said. "Can they go forward in time now and see if they're still here ten years from now? If they are, what chance do we have of driving them out?"

"That brings us to the key question," Nancy said gravely. "Tell them, Nelva."

"At first," Nelva began, "there was established what was believed to be a basic law—the inalterability of the future. And of the past, too. In your early twentieth century fiction there were time paradoxes advanced. You know the type; a man with a time machine goes back and kills his grandfather—when he was a boy—does that automatically cancel his being born? A man goes forward in time and sees himself killed in a train wreck on such and such a date, so when that time comes he doesn't take the train, thereby saving his life. It was early found that there are time quanta. In time travel you can't just stop anywhere like that and do things. When you start there is a minimum extent of time before you can come back into the general drift again."

"But we did," Joe objected. "In fact, we could go out right now and shoot ourselves so that we would now be dead several days."

"In the abstract, yes," Nelva agreed. "In practice, you would never accomplish it, because it didn't happen. I don't care how firmly you wanted to, or how carefully you worked it out, something would prevent it."

"O.K.," Joe said, laughing comfortably. "I won't do it then—just to keep you happy."

"That's nice of you," Nelva smiled. "But the firmly established laws of the inviolability of time lately received a setback. One of the major research projects of the Vargians is exploration of the future. Just a few years ago there were discovered what were thought to be errors of previous explorers. For example, an explorer reported in 1970 that on January first, 2025 a certain event will take place or is taking place. An explorer from 1999 in going forward finds that there was an error—it took place earlier or later—or not at all.

"With one or two such cases it could be called error; but the cases are mounting up. In fact, they're increasing. There's enough data now to form a probability equation that has almost been accepted in place of the old law of unchangeability. That equation, carried down to its limit, the present time, says that events of tomorrow have an almost equal chance of being different than those observed for tomorrow from twenty years back."

"But how can that be?" Ray asked. "If you go forward and see something actually happen, it—it just happens that way, doesn't it? It's not a dream. It's real. If it isn't, then all time travel is just a vivid dream, and Joe and I are sleeping it off back in 1950."

"I hope not," Joe said, looking at Nancy brazenly. She stuck out her tongue at him.

"That's what they can't understand," Nelva said. "And they can't decide whether it's something new, or a principle that's just newly discovered."

"Is there a difference?" Joe asked.

"You'll see the difference in a minute, Joe," Nancy said. "Want some more coffee?"

"Sure," Joe said.

"Here's the difference," Nelva said. "If it's just a newly discovered law that has always existed, then it held true back in Varmour—but records of similar studies back in that period don't show it. That would be according to the probability law too, because study of even the records of that time would now be in the certainty category.

"But if it's something new, it means that there is an entirely new force coming into the picture that was not present before. Then the constants of the probability equation alter in significance. They become the secondary variables expressing the intrusion of this new force into the time stream. Then, instead of the equation saying that the closer you get to the present the more unpredictable events are, it says that at some time soon events will be entirely different than they are as we observe them from the present."

"I think I see what you mean," Ray said slowly. "You mean that they can go forward in time from right now and see Vargians still quietly running things, but with this new element in the picture it may turn out they aren't there at all when the time stream reaches that point."

"Exactly," Nelva said. "And that's why they fear me. They rightly conclude that I have brought this new factor into the picture. It takes away the certainty of future events, and they can't see what's coming and be prepared to counter it."

"Whew," Joe exclaimed. "It puts them in the same boat as people without time travel. They can't buy tomorrow's paper and see who won the race, and come back and bet on the winner, because the winner might lose."

"Wait a minute, Joe," Ray said. "I want to get things straightened out in my mind. I'm not sure I understand it all yet. The way I understand it, the Vargians have been in the habit of systematically exploring the future, say twenty years ahead, and keeping records so when they reach that period they know from the records what is going to happen tomorrow."

"Roughly, that's the idea," Nelva admitted. "Though it would be more accurate to include the forty and sixty year jumps too. Then you get a better understanding of it. Then you can see how the discrepancies came to light in ordinary routine work. The records of the year two thousand that was made by the twenty-years-in-the-future department in 1980 were checked against those of the same year, made in 1960 by the forty-years-in-the-future department. The lack of agreement was too great for just error."

"Then," Ray said. "If that's so, a year from now they'll have a third check, the events themselves."

"That's right," Nelva agreed. "And it's the big unknown, because time travel machines as the Vargians have them can't jump such a short distance."

"All right," Ray said. "Tell me this. Were any of the events of 1999 or previous years different than they were observed by observers from, say, twenty years ago?"

"I'll show you one," Nelva said quietly. "Just a minute till I come back."

She left the room. A moment later she was back with an envelope from which she extracted three newspaper clippings. Ray and Joe examined them interestedly. They seemed the same at first glance. All three were dated July 7, 1950. Two of them were the same, word for word. The third was three lines shorter than the other two.

Inked in over each clipping was a date. The dates were August 9, 1930, July 30, 1950, and June 5, 1974.

The ones from 1930 and 1950 reported the mysterious explosion in which Ray and Joe had been. It gave their names and reported them as having been seriously injured. The one with 1974 inked over it reported that no one was injured.

Joe whistled in amazement. Ray frowned in thought. "Now read these," Nelva said quietly, handing them three other clippings. The printed date on each was July 13, 1950, with the three inked-in dates over each clipping.

Two of them reported Ray's and Joe's death that day from injuries sustained in the mysterious explosion of July seventh. The third reported that the two had been missing since the mysterious explosion and were being sought by the police for questioning.

"And now this," Nelva said, handing them a lone clipping.

Its date line was November 12, 1950. It reported that Einar Gunnarson had leased a garage building to two men and received three months rent in advance. When the three months were up and he had received no more rent, he went to the garage building to see about it. The building was empty, but there was some sort of strange distortion existing inside the building. Gunnarson had reported it to the police and advanced the theory that the two young men wanted to buy the property and had rented it in order to set up the strange disturbance so that no one else could use it, and he would be forced to sell it at a low figure.

"That clipping has no corresponding one for 1950 or 1930," Nelva said. "It's from 1974."

"So that's how it works," Ray said. "In the first two Joe and I got killed. In the third you warned me, and we escaped. But how can that be? It's—it's like we lived a plurality and one split off from another so that in the explosion I became two, and one of me died."

"No, that isn't it," Nelva said. "I think I can make you understand by something that's going on right now. Right this minute you are here, and also in the city doing exactly the things you remember having done in full consciousness several days ago at this instant. Last night you managed to contact yourself and become, in effect, a part of your subconscious. The whole thing is a phenomenon of consciousness and a property of consciousness. The universe is at least five-dimensional, but consciousness is three- dimensional. If your conscious mind were truly four-dimensional instead of being three and moving forward in the fourth as a 'flat' wave front, you would be equally aware in both places, and in all space locations in every instant of time in between.

"So, the way I see it," she concluded. "The awareness in your body in the city right now is another wave-front of consciousness travelling along the same four-dimensional route you yourself traveled not long ago."

"For the first time *I'm* beginning to see it," Joe said. "It's like a wave breaking against a shore. One wave comes in and breaks, but another wave is going over the same course. Napoleon at Waterloo is a four dimensional shore of an ocean, and at regular intervals consciousness-waves travel up and pass over it; and we could travel back and merge with the current wave and go along with it."

"Very much like that," Nelva said. "Only now the contours of the channels can be changed—from the fifth dimension." She saw the blank look on Joe's face. "Look at it this way, Joe. Consider time, ordinary time, as a point moving at a constant speed in a straight line. The straight line is the time-continuum, and the point is the present."

"O.K.," Joe said. "I got it."

"And the moving point is conscious awareness," Nelva went on. "There can be other points ahead and behind it on the line, travelling along at the same speed, which is a universal constant like the speed of light."

"That's clear," Joe agreed. "And time travel consists of jumping ahead and slipping in at another of those moving points."

"Basically; yes," Nelva said. "Now consider the line as the continuity of events through which the point of consciousness travels. That point moves along the line, rather than generating the line. The line isn't altered by the passage of the point. In fact, from the laws of physics, there's no way of altering that line—curving it from its normal straightness—from within the line itself."

"Got it," Joe exclaimed. "If we consider that line as being four-dimensional space-time, then the only way real events can be altered is by getting outside the line into another dimension and pushing. That means the fifth dimension. Do you see what I mean?"

"Right," Nelva said. "And up until I discovered how to move into the fifth dimension by the time travel principle, the line remained straight. Now the picture is this: one moving point passes a given point on the line while it's straight. Then I curve the line a little and the next follows the curve. So I was actually bending the space-time line when I gave the warning from outside it and enabled you two to escape the explosion. But the day is passing—I want to introduce you to our fellow researchers and—well, I might as well warn you; we plan on revamping you two into something like supermen. Can you take it?"

"As long as it doesn't make me too good to associate with Nancy I don't mind," Joe said. "But there's an old saying that the best way to get rid of a guy is to kick him upstairs."

"Nothing like that," Nelva said.

"I want to hear Nancy say it," Joe said.

"O.K., Joe," Nancy said, laughing. "I'll still love you, darling."

"Fine," Joe grinned. Then he looked into her eyes, and added quietly, "I hope when this is all over you can say that again—and mean it."

CHAPTER SEVENTEEN

"YOU SURE BELIEVE in scattering things over the landscape," Joe complained. "Why couldn't you have clustered your building all in one spot, since you don't have any crowding?"

"We didn't build the houses and buildings we have," Nelva said.

"What? They were already here?" Ray exclaimed.

"They were 'where' they are," Nelva answered. "Mine and Nancy's house, for example, is one we 'picked up' back in 1953. We merely built in the right design of solenoids to 'move' it forward in time and just far enough out of phase with the time front—or into the fifth dimension—to be where and when we wanted it. It created quite a stir." She chuckled at the memory, Nancy joining in. "There was quite a write-up in the papers about the mysterious theft of an entire house including the full concrete basement, leaving just a hole in the ground. And the owners—that's us—disappeared along with it. I believe in your day before the full extent of reality was known they called such occurrences 'Fortean data,' didn't they?"

"Yes," Ray said. "There's thousands of examples of mysterious disappearances like that—and also materializations of both common and strange things."

"The house remained 'where' it was," Nancy cut in. "We are still in the same place with it."

"And all our other buildings are the same," Nelva went on. "We bought them and moved them out of their timeline, but they had to stay put in space relative to their surroundings. That's why they're scattered out. Another thing, we had to pick them far apart and in different years so it wouldn't seem to all be done at once, though we actually accomplished it all in just one week, in terms of our own conscious time lapse."

She guided the car up a driveway and stopped in front of a neat, one-story brick building.

"This is the big project," she said. "You'll meet Dr. Osburn and Dr. Scott. I think they're here."

They climbed out of the car and crossed to the building, which was an island structure of solidity in the sea of shadow and light shapes that made up the rest of their surroundings. Joe and Ray were getting used to this dualism.

"The door even has a lock on it," Joe said humorously.

"We got it with the lock on," Nancy said. "But we don't need to lock it. There's nobody around but just us people."

"Then what's that?" Joe said, pointing.

They all turned to look where he pointed. It was a rabbit, patiently trying to nibble grass that slipped through its teeth without so much as bending.

"Oh," Nancy said in pretended anger at the rabbit. "It would make me out a liar. That's one of Dr. Scott's experimental animals."

"Must have gotten loose," Nelva said. "Poor thing. I'll bet it's hungry." She walked toward it slowly while it watched her, wiggling its nose in slow thoughtfulness.

As she leaned over to pick it up, it decided to become alarmed. Its hind legs sank into the ground as it jumped, having the effect of loosely packed sawdust. It landed on its side less than a foot away and Nelva grabbed it.

She stood up, cuddling it in her arm and rubbing behind its ears to calm it down.

"What kind of animals did you have back in the days of Varmour, Nelva?" Ray Bradley asked. "Certainly not the ones we have today—nor even the same plants."

"You're right," Nelva said. "We brought some of them forward with us, of course. Housepets, a few of the more interesting ones for the zoos."

The rabbit in her arms suddenly dropped right through them to land on the ground, a form of shadow and light. It stood there a brief moment, then bounded away.

"That explains how it got out," Nancy said. She saw the dumfounded looks on Ray's and Joe's faces and laughed.

"It's one of the experiments on direct nervous control of time travel," Nelva explained. "It must have changed over while Dr. Scott or one of his assistants was carrying it, because its cage is really a double cage, the other-solid half being a box buried in a small hillock that's in the same space as the cages, so it won't be noticed on the other side. It takes time for the animals to learn how to deliberately change their state."

"That one must know how," Nancy said. "When it was excited it didn't, but after it calmed down it remembered how, and escaped from your arms, Nelva."

"It certainly did," Nelva said. She opened the front door of the building and walked in, Nancy, Ray, and Joe behind her.

The interior was clean. That was the first impression it gave. The cleanliness of new paint not yet dirty or washed, of sun-washed air, of antiseptics, and of men with white clothes and rubber gloves.

They were in an empty outer office. In front of them was the open doorway of a hall that ran the length of the building, and it was from this hall that the impressions of the whole building came.

Nelva led the way into the hall and halfway down its length, where she turned into a doorway that opened on a large room that might have been a modern doctor's office suite with all the partitions removed.

Two gray haired men were standing by a window talking in low voices as they entered. They looked up, a smile of welcome appearing on their faces.

"Good morning, Nelva, Nancy," they said. "And these two young men are Ray Bradley and Joe Ashford."

"Yes," Nancy said. "This is Joe, Dr. Scott, Dr. Osburn. And this is Ray."

The two doctors shook hands solemnly with Ray and Joe.

Dr. Scott had a tight, almost parchment-like face with a sparse sprinkling of freckles. He was the habitually thin type—the scholar. Dr. Osburn wore his skin loosely, showing signs of former heaviness that had been lost with the passing of the years.

"We have something in common that I'll bet you haven't thought of," the latter said with a twinkle as he shook hands with Ray. "I was born in 1925. You must have been born about the same year, considering your apparent age and the fact that you skipped half a century of time."

"That's the year of my birth," Ray exclaimed, startled. "Well, I'll be darned. I'm twenty-five and you're seventy-five, and we were born the same year…"

"Maybe I can have my wish," Joe spoke up. "I really would like to drop in on myself and talk over old times together."

"Don't mind Joe," Ray said with mock apology. "He's a little cracked from all this time travel."

"Not at all," Dr. Scott replied seriously. "I think he has a sense of humor. Not cracked, as you call it, at all."

Ray and Joe lifted their eyebrows at each other.

"We found one of the rabbits outside," Nelva changed the subject. "I caught him but he changed state and got away."

"Ah, that must be the one that escaped yesterday when I was carrying him over to the table to examine him," Dr. Osburn said. "Too bad. We spent a lot of time and trouble on him. We'll never be able to get him again."

"He served his purpose, anyway," Dr. Scott said cheerfully. "We learned a lot from him." He smiled at Joe and Ray. "Experience that we will need to operate on you two."

"Operate?" Joe said, dismayed. "Oh no you don't. I'm not a rabbit. Anyway, there's nothing wrong with me."

"You don't understand," Dr. Scott said. "We're going to make you two able to travel in time or out of time by control directly from the brain—just like the rabbit."

Ray and Joe turned and looked at Nelva questioningly. She nodded with an air of finality.

"That's what we were talking about when we said you were to be made into supermen," she said. "You don't need to be afraid. It won't be dangerous. And it's absolutely vital for our plans if we hope to succeed."

"Who's afraid?" Joe said, looking doubtfully at Dr. Scott's hands with their slight though perpetual tremble.

"Nothing to be afraid of at all, Joe," Dr. Scott said calmly. "And don't worry. We aren't going to do it just yet. Not until we make exhaustive tests of your anatomy and nervous system, and you thoroughly understand what it's all about."

"What do you do?" Ray spoke up. "Attach control wires to nerves?"

"That's exactly right, Ray," the doctor said. "We do it in two stages. The first is what you might consider pre-education of the nervous system. We operate and bring out the nerve ends that are to do the controlling, and attach them to devices that do something harmless—like operating a light switch or ringing a bell. Something tangible but harmless. Then you have a period of learning to do what you intend to do, until we're sure you won't get confused. After that we connect the wires to the solenoids and bury them in your body at strategic points for full field coverage. When it's all over there's nothing to indicate they are there, and by mind alone you can go forward or backward or sideways in time.

"But come. We would like you to see our work. The animals we've perfected our techniques on. The instrument lab where Dr. Osburn and his helpers make the solenoids and test them. Everything."

"Oh. Then you're not a surgeon, Dr. Osburn?" Ray asked.

"Oh yes," the doctor replied. "I developed into a specialist—a research surgeon. My specialty is joining the animate and the inanimate. Substances that living tissue will grow onto and not come loose, and things allied to that. It's quite a field—and very necessary when you have the problem of peppering the human body with inanimate solenoids connected to nerves and operated from brain impulses. Dr. Scott does the actual surgery, and don't let the nervous palsy of his hands dismay you. With a scalpel in his fingers they become steady as a rock."

"O.K., I'm convinced," Joe said.

The doctors led the way into an adjoining room that was fourteen feet wide and at least thirty feet long. It was an eerie place. Ghost-like weeds and grass grew on a shadow hill that rose head high. The doctors led them around the base of the mound.

"We can't walk into it without going fully out of phase," Dr. Scott said. "You could by pushing against the ceiling, but you can see the animals in their pens without going to that trouble. As you can see, some of them are in our phase, and some of them are in the solid world. They're learning. Some of them have already learned, and switch back and forth at will. That rabbit that got away could do that, though we hadn't thought he could yet or we would have taken the precaution of putting him to sleep with gas before taking him out of his pen."

"What's that animal?" Ray asked, pointing to a strange one.

"Oh, that," Dr. Scott said. "That's the ancestor of the horse."

"They were as plentiful in Varmour," Nancy said, "as your wild rabbits are in America. Quite a pest, in fact. And, like your rabbits, we have domestic strains that we raise for eating. Naturally the Vargians brought some with them into the modern world."

"You eat horse meat?" Joe said, shocked.

"Not the modern horse," Nancy laughed gleefully. "The little ones are fine grained and as tasty as your rabbits are. Incidentally—that was one of the biggest surprises for the Vargians, to find the eventual evolution of the horse into the modern racing strains and the stocky work strains used in Europe. Also, to find that modern scientists had found remains of the former species and recognized it as the ancestor."

Joe and Ray studied the animals with interest. They were about the size of a small dog, their bodies larger in proportion to their legs than in modern horses, their feet quite different. They were all colors like cats. They might not have even remotely seemed to be horses except for the fact that their faces were unmistakable.

"Now, if you've seen enough here," Dr. Osburn said cheerfully. "Let me show you my kingdom of wire and plastic."

"Lead us to it," Ray said. "That's something I at least can understand."

Dr. Osburn led them across the hall. Here it was one vast room in which were benches and instruments on every side.

"Every conceivable experiment goes on here," Dr. Osburn explained enthusiastically, his eyes youthfully alive. "Some of them sour on us, but not all. For example, we've tried going farther into the fifth dimension, but it's ticklish. If you just send solenoids out they drop toward the center of the Earth." He chuckled. "So far none of us has had guts enough to risk going ourselves. There might not be any way to get back up."

He led the way to a long table on which several panels gleamed.

"This is the real project," he said. "We make alloys of slightly out of phase substances and test them here. Get some interesting results, too. Materials that are solid on every plane. In other words, time-wide. Look at this one." He pointed to a cube of copper. "That doesn't look it, of course, but it's our diving board into the fifth dimension. The parts co-exist in three dimensional space, but in the fifth dimension that cube is the equivalent of several feet long, just like a diving board stuck out over a swimming pool. It's made by alloying a succession of coppers slightly out of phase, one after another.

"We use it to send things into the fifth dimension. We set them on it and start them, and when they reach the end they drop through, and on down to the Earth's center, so far as we know."

Ray reached toward it, then looked at Dr. Osburn questioningly.

"Go ahead and pick it up, Ray," the doctor said. "It won't hurt you. In fact, we've found by spectroscopic study from different degrees of materialization that most matter has a lot of out-of-phase material in it."

Ray picked up the copper tube. It was normally heavy. In no way could he distinguish it from ordinary copper.

"It seems like normal copper," he said.

"There's only one way you could detect the difference," Dr. Osburn said. "If you took a slice off of it and weighed it, and then dissolved it in acid, you'd find that about a third of it had mysteriously become lost. That would be the out of phase parts that didn't combine. Some of them would be left, but some would drop down in the liquid and lodge in the test tube or beaker or whatever you used to hold the acid. Another way, if you wanted to get the equipment, is to shoot its atoms through a cyclotron. It would give an abnormally high concentration of mesons, because that classification includes a lot of slightly out of phase ordinary matter."

"So that's a cube of copper about an inch and a half on each side," Joe said. "And several feet 'long' in the fifth dimension. Like taking a wire and stretching it in the fifth dimension. Is there any way of telescoping it back into just three dimensions? Or, if you put it in a five dimensional field, will it remain the same, so when you brought it back it would be unchanged?"

"Ah ha," Dr. Osburn said with a cunning twinkle. "You're sharp. You've guessed at our top secret, our time trap. But I'm not going to tell you a thing about it until after your overhauling on the other side of the hall. So, for about three days, you can just puzzle about it."

CHAPTER EIGHTEEN

THERE ARE SOME experiences in life that, however fantastic, never lose their flavor of reality. There are others that seem unreal—a dream—while they are happening and after. There are still others that, however small in scope, seem to enwrap one inexorably, with the impersonal inevitableness of a landslide from which there is no escape, or the inescapable numbing shock of oncoming car headlights in the instant before head-on collision.

You are perhaps walking along a grassy ledge, more than wide enough for safety so that you don't have to think about the hundred foot sheer drop from it to the valley floor you just came from. To your right as you stroll along, the steep slope climbs upward and upward toward the clouds. Then, suddenly, you hear a rattle—an unreal rattle that might be a drum, a tin can, or rocks rattling together.

You look up the slope and see the unreality of the landslide, an avalanche of dirt and rocks and uprooted plants rushing down—still hundreds of yards away. There is time to run back, to run forward. But no, that unreality is a broad sweeping tide that extends both ways, cutting you off. You turn this way and that. Every possible move is death. So at last you stand there, accepting it. There is nothing else you can do.

Ray and Joe behind their calm, even jesting exteriors, went through much the same series of emotional stages. It began with the same abruptness after they left the lab building and were led to a nearby house and shown to a room with two hospital beds—and calmly told by Nelva and Nancy that the party was over. It was time now to settle down and get ready for the first operation.

"It has to be done right away," Nelva informed them. "There will be long hours of learning to ring bells and flash lights through neural relays—more long hours of getting used to the ability to jump around in five dimensions by thought alone—and all that has to be over by the time this time-stream catches up with the time you first met us in that roadhouse."

And so it began. Going without dinner—and considering and rejecting the alternatives. Opiate and restless dozing under opiate that suddenly robs you of those precious last hours by plunging you into deep sleep so that the next instant it is morning and the dread moment is upon you rather than hours away as it was a fleeting thought before, in the quiet of the night. Cowardly thoughts of escape that must be concealed beneath calm faces lest Nelva and Nancy might suspect you're just a blown egg…lights and the ether mask looming over you.

"Breathe deeply now." And Dr. Scott's face looking down at you—a different face now. That of a man about to do what he lives to do—no longer an old man. A surgeon in the operating room.

"You are back in bed," you think. "But what's holding you so still?" You open your eyes and see the straps that imprison your wrists, the dozens of tubes that disappear into your flesh, with wires running out of them to red lights and blue lights and little plastic boxes with buzzers visible inside them. And one of the blue lights winks on, stares at you, then goes out. And you know that somewhere in your mind you did that yourself—by thought.

Eternal, thirsty hours, during which you learn to turn on all the blue lights at once—except two, then one, and finally all of them flash on when you will it. And red lights. And you know there are two kinds of bells. You learn it all. Red lights. Blue lights. High pitched bells. Lower pitched bells. Red lights, blue lights, high notes, low notes. Red-materialize, blue-dematerialize, do-go-ahead-in-time, sol-go-back-in-time.

"That's bad. A red light lit when you rang the low-note buzzers. Try again. It's got to become automatic and infallible. Relax. Relax."

And at last you open your eyes. The tubes with their wires, and the lights and buzzers are gone. You feel relaxed. Nelva and Nancy are smiling down at you.

Suddenly you remember. You're afraid of what might happen. Then abruptly the fear is gone. There were too many hours of drilling and training. There's nothing to be afraid of—only now the gun is loaded. No blanks. No red lights and blue lights and buzzers.

"Stay put, you," Nelva jeers good naturedly, and you realize you've been switching around in all five dimensions. But how could she do the same?

You sit up in bed as the startling truth hits you, and wonder why it wasn't obvious all the time.

"You can do it too," Ray exclaimed.

"Of course," Nelva murmured. Her eyes softened. "There are four of us now. You and I, and Joe and Nancy."

Suddenly Ray knew how lonesome and alone Nelva had been. He sat up in bed and held out his arms. She crept into them.

"The Alchemy of the gods," Ray murmured.

"What?" Nelva asked dreamily.

"Nothing, darling," Ray said. "It was just a way of saying we've found each other at last."

"Yes," Nelva said, firmly pushing away from him.

"And now we must get ready for the big moment. Here everything is five-dimensionally solid. This is really two houses in the same space, two beds in the same space, permanent, so that when you awakened you wouldn't run into trouble before you got your wits about you.

"We have approximately eight hours for you and Joe to learn all the little things you must watch out for in switching around, and to get your sea legs. We have to be back at the roadhouse at the moment we vanished, because our plans begin from there. Also you and Joe have to learn our plan and your part in it."

CHAPTER NINETEEN

CRAIG BLANNING, with his features carefully altered so that neither Ray nor Joe would have recognized him, drove swiftly after the car in which Ray Bradley and Joe Ashford were going to their rendezvous with Nelva. The three young ladies and two men in the car with him were all members of the Custodians.

The car radio brought frequent terse reports of the path Ray and Joe were taking, sent by hidden highway police patrol officers.

Thus it was that when Ray and Joe decided—apparently on the spur of the moment—to stop and have a drink at the next roadhouse, Craig was a mere half mile behind, and able to drive in and park, and enter the place at the same time as those two.

He had a brief moment of panic when Ray bumped him at the entrance, but Ray gave no indication of having recognized him.

Inside, he and his party took a table near the two, where they could survey the patrons without seeming to do so.

It was then that he hit on the idea of taking their car away from them. He outlined the plan to one of his men. When Ray rose and went toward the men's room the man followed him, returning with the key to the car and a dazed look. It had been too easy.

"Well," Craig said. "Then this must be where he intends to meet Nelva. Just in case, though, we'll go ahead with it. Take the car, and if this isn't the place we'll manage to talk them into riding with us where they're going."

"Damn," the man muttered. "I'd hoped to be in the action."

After he departed Craig watched Ray and Joe covertly. He followed their gaze when they spied the two girls, and recognized them instantly as Nelva and Nancy.

As Ray and Joe rose from their stools at the bar and crossed the floor leisurely, Craig debated whether to turn the battery of paralysis ray pistols of his group on the two girls at once or wait. He decided to wait until Nelva and Nancy were off guard during the first moments of meeting Ray and Joe.

At the moment Nelva put her hand on Ray's arm Craig decided it was time to act.

"Now," he muttered. As one, he and his three companions rose, drawing out their paralysis pistols, and pointed them at the four in the booth twenty feet away. As Craig pressed the stud of his pistol he saw the four figures become shadowy and vanish.

Instantly he was across the room, taking a small, compact object from his pocket as he ran to the now empty booth. When he reached it he laid the object on one of the seats where the four had been sitting and pulled a pin.

The object was deceptive looking. It was a small bomb, able to follow an induced time stream and explode when it met solidity.

It was his ace in the hole, guaranteed to follow Nelva to whatever time she went and destroy her. He waited for it to vanish on its pursuit. Instead, it remained there.

Craig leaped back in alarm, realizing that at the end of ten seconds its fuse would become activated in preparation detonation, and if it were not gone in time it would blow up right there.

His thoughts were struggling with the problem even as he tried to escape the blast. Why hadn't the bomb followed the four? How had they all vanished without benefit of time travel equipment?

The blast caught him and flung him backward into people seated at tables. He lost consciousness.

When he came to, the sound of sirens dying down outside was the first thing he became aware of. He lay quietly, exploring himself in search of injury. When he finally moved a little, tentatively, he decided he hadn't been hurt—probably just knocked out by the explosion or by hitting a table.

He went over to the shambles that had been the booth. There was little left. At his back he heard the screams of the injured. The police joined him quickly. Other police were restoring order to the place, shouting for people to calm down and move back, telling the injured to be quiet until the ambulances arrived.

"Look," Craig said urgently to the officer in charge, showing him his badge of authority in his billfold. "Keep everyone away from this spot where the explosion occurred, and get me back to town as quickly as possible. I've got to report to Vargian headquarters at once."

The badge brought immediate action.

"Stay here until I get back," Craig ordered his assistants. He introduced them to the officer in charge. A moment later he was scrunched forward beside the driver of the patrol car, speeding toward the city with screaming siren at three hundred miles an hour.

Just before they entered the city limits he managed to get through to Vargian headquarters and tell them briefly the outcome of their attempt.

Fifteen minutes later he was at the foot of the table around which the Vargians sat, gravely listening and questioning him.

"You say the tracer bomb just stayed there?" one of them asked.

"That's correct," Craig said.

"There can be only one explanation," another said slowly. "It also accounts for our not being able to locate Nelva during all the time we've searched for her. She's discovered some field of reality we haven't as yet reached with our own devices."

"That must be it," another agreed. "Mathematics has always predicted that there would be others, other dimensions. Our job now is to get equipment out there and pick up the trail. Regardless of what type of mechanism she used, there will be the track of the force field there at the instant prior to their disappearance—and our instruments can follow it and determine its nature."

"We'd better hurry," another said. "There are ways of confusing a time-track so it can't be followed. Also, if she has gone to an unknown aspect of reality it may be that she can be aware of what we do—even be present here right now."

"Our extra-temporal eye won't help us," another said dryly as most of the Vargians began to look around uneasily.

Suddenly every voice in the room stilled. A panel on the wall had come to life. On it was the face that looked down on the people all over the city from the hundreds of monitored spyscreens, the face of Vargia, the Queen. Only in this screen it was not still, but alive.

As one man everyone present in the room stood and bowed, remaining that way. Vargia looked out at them over the two-way television, her face a mixture of temperaments, as her nature had always been since birth.

"So you *almost* caught her," her voice said quietly. She noted, with apparent satisfaction the trembling of shoulders of these leaders, and of Craig. Craig, she knew as a Vargian noble who, because he was second born, had been denied the extra-temporal eye so that he, like her sisters, could never assume the leadership of his line.

"I've been listening to your discussions," Vargia went on finally. "Why didn't you try to kill Nelva before she had a chance to steal those two from 1950 away from you? The best she could have hoped for then would have been escape—to try again to reach her object of affection. Now there's nothing—except perhaps a faint time track into a realm of physics we know nothing about."

"But we'll have other chances," Craig said eagerly. "With him she has what she needs to carry out her plans. We can get her when she appears."

"Nonsense," Vargia said. "Her plans don't depend on a stupid savage from half a century ago. It's obvious to me that she's fallen in love with him. He was the best bait you'll ever have to catch her—and she got away with him. *Bah!*"

"I have incurred your displeasure," Craig said woodenly.

"You have," Vargia said coldly.

The Vargians in the room raised their eyes expectantly, and watched in fascination as they saw Craig draw out his ray tube and change the adjustment to "lethal."

His face was pale as he raised the tube to his forehead. His finger whitened on the fire stud.

But suddenly one of the Vargians jumped toward him excitedly. At the same instant Craig's ray tube flew from his grasp, it flew through the air to the Vargian, and Ray Bradley materialized beside Craig, reaching toward him, to grasp his arm and draw him across into the time stream.

The Vargian fumbled hastily to reset the ray intensity to half strength, then turned it on Ray, freezing his muscles.

Ray tried to take his finger from the switch in his pocket so he could vanish. He couldn't. Sweat stood out on his forehead from the effort.

The Vargian, his eyes flashing with excitement, held the paralysis ray on him steadily.

The other Vargians now had ray tubes out and ready. Their eyes roamed the room expectantly. But now a tinkle of laughter came from queen Vargia on the screen.

"Nelva will not be fool enough to try to rescue him," she said. "*She* knows the danger of your extra-temporal eye that can see events about to take place, even though her lover didn't— the fool. He has probably cost her the entire battle, since she will risk everything to rescue him." Her voice became coolly authoritative. "Slash his clothes and discover the devices that enabled him to materialize. His hand in his pocket—it's probably on a safety device that controls the mechanism."

Craig Blanning carefully slit the pocket. There was nothing.

"Then bring him to me, quickly," Vargia commanded. "And be careful. Nelva might attempt a rescue if you relax even for an instant."

"This is it," Ray thought to himself as he was ushered into the vast audience chamber of the queen of the Vargians.

He marveled at the vastness of the place. The floor covered a full acre. The walls were of tremendously thick marble that rose twenty feet. The vast dome ceiling arched upward, supported only by the walls with no supporting pillars anywhere on the vast floor expanse.

It was architecture such as had never been attempted by man up to 1950. There was grudging admiration in Ray's eyes as he saw the queen standing on a dais at the far end of the hall, diminutive in the vast space, yet gaining stature by the very fact that she could dominate it—be the focus of its greatness.

As her features slowly enlarged with the decreasing distance, he saw that if her beauty and strangeness had arrested him so precipitously when he first saw it in that drugstore the first time, it was even more striking now in animation and life.

Her central eye was a gleaming, smoky jewel. Her features were a contrast of conflicting emotion—superhuman. Queenly and deadly. He realized he was facing a woman who could and probably had—many times—indulged in the lust of killing. She had the power and the authority to be a law unto herself.

At last he was at the foot of the dais where she stood before the background of her throne. The Vargians who had been carrying him set him on his feet and held him up. The paralysis ray still played on him, holding his muscles rigid, yet he knew that he could slip away—vanish beyond the range of the rays, merely by willing it.

With his new power he could not be held in any prison nor by any force. But the Vargians about him didn't suspect that, nor did queen Vargia.

She now showed a gleaming, ornate paralysis gun. She turned it on him and ordered the Vargian to put his away.

Her eyes took on a gleam of sadism. She depressed the trigger more and more. Ray felt the tingle and torture of the force through his body. Sweat broke out from every pore. Still he withstood it, waiting. He knew that Vargia wouldn't kill him.

At last she relented, softening the ray to almost nothing. The sadism in her eyes changed to cold purpose.

"You will tell me the secret of the device by which Nelva and Nancy have escaped me," she said quietly. "If you do this quickly and willingly it will save you tortures and may bring rewards beyond your expectations."

This was the moment. Ray hesitated, making it last a second or two, thinking that there must be a sadistic streak in himself to relish so much what was about to happen.

"Perhaps," he said vaguely. "But first—look at this."

He raised his hand and pointed a finger at the nearest Vargian. He was one of those with white hair and a gleaming center eye. Slowly that eye dimmed.

In the space of a held breath it changed and diminished until it was nothing but smooth skin with no trace of the eye left. The forehead was that of an ordinary man.

There were gasps of horror all about him. Ray looked up at the queen. Her face was distorted with an indescribable horror, a terrible dread.

Suddenly she raised the paralysis gun and constricted her finger. But Ray had seen the move and vanished. Visible to him now were Nelva and Nancy and Joe, and the vast hall was a thing of shadow and unsolid light.

Also barely visible was the swath of Vargians and slaves that had been mowed down by the lethal intensity of the beam from Vargia's ray gun meant for him.

He leaped onto the dais and went to stand just behind the queen, bringing himself into almost three quarter phase with solidity.

"If you drop your ray gun and order your men to not try anything," he said, "I'll come back and finish my message."

Vargia hesitated, then obeyed, her face a mask of anger and hate.

Ray stepped down again and resumed his former position. Then suddenly the lights and shadows about him were solid once more, and the three, Nelva, Nancy, and Joe, vanished.

"What is your message?" Vargia asked frigidly.

"Simply this," Ray said. "You saw what I could do to an extra-temporal eye. I can do the same to yours. I'm not alone. You searched for devices concealed on me. You didn't find any because there aren't any. Yet I can jump forward or backward in time, seconds or hours or years. I can do it by willing it. I can do it while your paralysis ray guns hold me helpless, unable to move a muscle.

"I could have escaped any time I chose. I came willingly, in order to tell you what's in store for you, and all Vargians."

"But it isn't," Vargia replied. "The future shows no fate in store for us. Whatever you plan will fail."

"I think you know different," Ray said. "You know that even this meeting is different than it could be seen from twenty years back—and your scientists don't know why, nor what is going on."

"I have to admit that's true," Vargia said hesitantly. "All right, what's your message."

"To tell you of a time trap that's been laid," Ray said.

"A time trap?" Vargia echoed, puzzled.

"Three days from now," Ray went on. "Every Vargian will lose his third eye. It will become just ordinary flesh, as you saw just now. There is no way you can prevent it."

"But that's no threat," Vargia murmured. "We can get along without it."

"You will lose yours too," Ray said. He saw the look of fear appear on her face. "How many of your subjects will willingly stay and face losing their third eye?" he went on triumphantly. "Even *you* won't stay."

"Stay?" Vargia said, as if it were a new idea that hadn't occurred to her.

"You'll have to go back where you came from—to Varmour," Ray said. "If you don't—your subjects will without you. Sure, you can restore your third eye once I blot it out. But as quickly as you do it will be changed back into plain skin and bone again."

He looked around at the horrified Vargians.

"Are you convinced?" he asked. "Or do you want more demonstrations. Look at the one who's lost his third eye."

That Vargian stood as in a daze. There was shock and bewilderment on his face.

"I don't know how much that will affect his mind," Ray went on. "But obviously it's affected it more than I, who don't have the extra-temporal visual center, can imagine."

He turned back to the queen.

"Should I point my finger at *your* eye?" he challenged.

"No," Vargia exclaimed, stepping back and stumbling against her throne, sitting down. "Is—is there no alternative? I'll promise to restore democracy—give Americans equal rights with Vargians."

"No," Ray said. "I had a taste of being considered the inferior racially. There's no compromise. Get out. Go back in time to where you came from. I'm going now. In three days at twelve o'clock noon every Vargian left here will lose his extra-temporal eye."

He looked at queen Vargia, knowing that in another moment he would never see her again as she was now. Then he sent the mental commands to the solenoids buried in his body that sent him sideways in time to the phase in which his three companions waited for him.

CHAPTER TWENTY

THE HELICOPTER hovered almost stationary in the high atmosphere. In it were Ray, Joe, Nelva, and Nancy. They were watching the departure of the Vargians.

The Vargians were leaving swiftly. Ship after ship rose, to gather speed and suddenly vanish as, clear of all obstructions, they switched into time-drive and plunged backward through the centuries to the time they had left.

Other thousands were doing the same all over the United States. They were racing against time. Racing to save their third eye.

"It was so simple," Joe said quietly. "I sometimes wonder what good force is. You can always find a way to do things without violence if you think hard enough." He ruffled his fingers through Nancy's hair absently.

"There'll be a few Vargians who will stay," Nelva said. "Those like us who were never given the third eye. But they will mix with ordinary Americans and be just like any other foreigner coming to America."

"And we can keep the Custodians in line," Ray said. "If they don't carry out their pledge to restore democracy we can harass them into it."

"The four musketeers," Joe grinned.

"And we can have a grand time for the rest of our lives," Nancy said. "We can travel through all the dimensions and find the mysteries of the Universe that are hidden from us now."

"There's something we have to do before we do any of those things, though," Ray said. "Something, more important even than making sure that the last three-eyed Vargian leaves."

"What's that?" Nelva said, but from the light in her two eyes Ray knew she had guessed.

"Find a preacher," he answered.

THE END

If you've enjoyed this book, you will not want to miss these terrific titles...

ARMCHAIR SCI-FI & HORROR DOUBLE NOVELS, $12.95 each

D-101 **THE CONQUEST OF THE PLANETS** by John W. Campbell
THE MAN WHO ANNEXED THE MOON by Bob Olsen

D-102 **WEAPON FROM THE STARS** by Rog Phillips
THE EARTH WAR by Mack Reynolds

D-103 **THE ALIEN INTELLIGENCE** by Jack Williamson
INTO THE FOURTH DIMENSION by Ray Cummings

D-104 **THE CRYSTAL PLANETOIDS** by Stanton A. Coblentz
SURVIVORS FROM 9,000 B. C. by Robert Moore Williams

D-105 **THE TIME PROJECTOR** by David H. Keller, M.D. and David Lasser
STRANGE COMPULSION by Philip Jose Farmer

D-106 **WHOM THE GODS WOULD SLAY** by Paul W. Fairman
MEN IN THE WALLS by William Tenn

D-107 **LOCKED WORLDS** by Edmond Hamilton
THE LAND THAT TIME FORGOT by Edgar Rice Burroughs

D-108 **STAY OUT OF SPACE** by Dwight V. Swain
REBELS OF THE RED PLANET by Charles L. Fontenay

D-109 **THE METAMORPHS** by S. J. Byrne
MICROCOSMIC BUCCANEERS by Harl Vincent

D-110 **YOU CAN'T ESCAPE FROM MARS** by E. K. Jarvis
THE MAN WITH FIVE LIVES by David V. Reed

ARMCHAIR SCIENCE FICTION CLASSICS, $12.95 each

C-34 **30 DAY WONDER**
by Richard Wilson

C-35 **G.O.G. 666**
by John Taine

C-36 **RALPH 124C 41+**
by Hugo Gernsback

ARMCHAIR SCI-FI & HORROR GEMS SERIES, $12.95 each

G-11 **SCIENCE FICTION GEMS, Vol. Six**
Edmond Hamilton and others

G-12 **HORROR GEMS, Vol. Six**
H. P. Lovecraft and others

If you've enjoyed this book, you will not want to miss these terrific titles...

ARMCHAIR SCI-FI & HORROR DOUBLE NOVELS, $12.95 each

D-111 **THE MOON ERA** by Jack Williamson
REVENGE OF THE ROBOTS by Howard Browne

D-112 **SON OF THE BLACK CHALICE** by Milton Lesser
SENTRY OF THE SKY by Evelyn E. Smith

D-113 **OUTPOST ON THE MOON** by Joslyn Maxwell
POTENTIAL ZERO by S. J. Byrne

D-114 **OUTPOST INFINITY** by Raymond F. Jones
THE WHITE INVADERS by Ray Cummings

D-115 **TIME TRAP** by Rog Phillips
THE COSMIC DESTROYER by Alexander Blade

D-116 **THE OTHER SIDE OF THE MOON** by Edmond Hamilton
SECRET INVASION by Walter Kubilius

D-117 **DANGER MOON** by Frederik Pohl
THE HIDDEN UNIVERSE by Ralph Milne Farley

D-118 **THE WAILING ASTEROID** by Murray Leinster
THE WORLD THAT COULDN'T BE by Clifford D. Simak

D-119 **THE WHISPERING GORILLA** by Don Wilcox
RETURN OF THE WHISPERING GORILLA by David V. Reed

D-120 **SPECIAL EFFECT** by J. F. Bone
WARLORD OF KOR by Terry Carr

ARMCHAIR SCIENCE FICTION CLASSICS, $12.95 each

C-37 **THE GREEN MAN RETURNS**
by Harold M. Sherman

C-38 **THE SHAVER MYSTERY, Book Five**
by Richard S, Shaver

C-39 **MARS CHILD**
by Cyril Judd

ARMCHAIR MASTERS OF SCIENCE FICTION SERIES, $16.95 each

MS-9 **MASTERS OF SCIENCE FICTION AND FANTASY, Vol. Nine**
Poul Anderson, "The Star Beast" and other tales

MS-10 **MASTERS OF SCIENCE FICTION, Vol. Ten**
Robert Moore Williams, "Time Tolls for Toro" and other tales

BIG TIME WOMAN TROUBLE IN OUTER SPACE

Sam Barron and the crew of his spaceship returned to their home planet, only to find themselves jeered at, shot at, and made to feel unwelcome in the loudest, angriest way possible. Death seemed an inevitable outcome should they decide to stick around. What Sam and his crew soon found out was that all Earthmen had been exiled. The reason why? One lone man had decided to "rescue" a young (and ever so lovely) priestess of the Amazon women. However, unknown to this female opportunist was that his fair priestess also possessed an incredible power—a power potent enough to destroy an entire galaxy!

So Sam and his crew realized they had two choices: Leave home forever…or find the girl and bring her back. But finding the girl was not an easy task due to the assassins, mercenaries, and other parties in pursuit of the impetuous priestess. Who would find her first? And who, if anyone, could convince her to go back?

CAST OF CHARACTERS

SAM BARRON
He was forbidden to return to his home planet because of a woman. Well, maybe a man. Well…it was complicated

ARRIKON
This Altairan bounty hunter was darn good at his job, and once he saw the power of his prize, he was relentless.

RED DeWALT
All he had wanted was a good time with a good-looking lady—so why, for cryin' out loud, were people trying to kill him?

LARYL
Exceptionally powerful, but exceptionally young—she was not one to make a rational decision.

YBRA
Full of youthful exuberance, this guy was all gung-ho for travel and adventure—even the deadly kind.

JOE LUCICH
He was usually never one to duck a fight, but he was in on making sure everything got back to normal.

THE COSMIC DESTROYER

By
ALEXANDER BLADE

ARMCHAIR FICTION
PO Box 4369, Medford, Oregon 97504

CHAPTER ONE

SAM BARRON was not more than fifteen yards away from *Starlady* when the first explosive pellets whistled over his head, following an outburst of angry shouting from the crowd.

He had taken care not to get too far away. Barron had traded all his life in the Pleiades, first in his father's ship and then in his own *Starlady*—who was not a lady at all but a sloppy old bag with rust in her primary tubes and a rattle in every plate. He knew all the worlds of the Seven Sisters stars, and he knew this world Esha of the blue star Sirrit better than any of them. If he had a home planet and a people, they were here. So the wrongness had hit him like a wave the minute he stepped out of *Starlady*'s lock with Joe Lucich, the First Mate.

There was always a crowd gathered on the spaceport to welcome a trading ship, or any ship at all. The Eshans were natural greeters. But this crowd was different. It was huge—there must have been twelve or thirteen hundred strung out in a thick sort of crescent, all adults and mostly men, with their white crests blowing and nodding in the wind. The women, about twenty of them wearing the black leotard of one of the amazon societies, stood together in a compact bunch a little ahead and outside of the crowd. They were armed with EP rifles. And all of them, men and women, were silent.

"What's it all about?" Joe Lucich had asked. "They act like they thought we had smallpox aboard."

Barron had said, "I don't know. But we'll soon find out."

And he had walked with Lucich out across the landing field, toward the low flat building of the port authority, with the long storage sheds beyond it. But he had walked slowly, because the crowd was between them and the buildings and he did not think it was there by accident.

"Why the Goon Girls?" Joe had muttered, looking at the amazons. "They're always off being holy somewhere, except when they're on business."

"They look," Barron had said, "as though they're on business now."

Then there was the sudden furious roar from the crowd, and the black-clad women shifted their ranks. Their rifles glinted brightly in the hot blue noon.

Sam Barron grabbed at Lucich and they both dropped.

The first fusillade went over them and popped with vicious flesh-bursting little cracks against *Starlady*'s hull or on the hard-fused ground. They got up and ran for the ship, bending low, while the amazons reloaded. They ran with the amazing speed of men whose lives are riding on their heels. The second fusillade was just a second too late.

"Close the lock!" Barron bellowed.

Somebody jumped to obey. Strings of firecrackers were still exploding against the hull. Barron ran into the control room with Lucich at his heels. He could hear Lucich breathing, panting like a dog, and he knew he was doing the same thing. The glare of the blue sun outside had been hot, but not hot enough to make him sweat the way he was sweating. He was shocked and angry, as though his best friend had turned on him savagely and without warning. He looked out the port.

The crowd had broken. It was spilling out over the landing field, a spate of lithe tall running forms and waving fists and white crests like battle-plumes, with the black shapes of the amazons scattered among them.

Old Viji, a seven-fingered humanoid from the other side of the Pleiades who had almost an esper linkage with drive-mechanisms, said dryly, "It looks like they're going to get you, Sam, one way or another. What did you do the last time you were here?"

Barron shook his head, watching the crowd.

"You, Joe?"

"Not one damned thing." Suddenly Lucich turned, his face crimson with rage. "But I'm going to do something now. I'm going to teach 'em they can't try to kill me and get away with it."

He flung himself into the pilot's seat and reached for the controls.

"Here," said Barron, "what are you doing?"

"Give 'em a blast," said Lucich, shaking with anger. "They want killing, okay. I'll give 'em some!"

"Get away from there," Barron said.

Lucich ignored him. His big hands reached for the lateral jet controls.

Barron swore. He knocked Lucich bodily out of the seat and stood over him with his fist raised.

"Anybody gets killed around here it'll be you," said Barron. He was shaking too. "What do you want to do, get us all hung?"

Lucich glowered, wiping his mouth with the back of his hand. But his gaze dropped and he muttered, "All right, all right. But I still say they got no right to—"

"Here comes Hlann," said Viji.

Barron joined him at the port. A small ancient jeep, painted with silver paint and adorned with flags, was zigzagging through the crowd. Beside the driver a long lean man was standing up and gesticulating at the people as he passed them.

"About time," said Barron. "Somebody must have hauled him out of bed." Hlann was Port Authority, and on this starport he had plenty of spare time. He spent most of it sleeping.

Barron went down the corridor to the airlock, telling Lucich to come with him. He did not want to leave Lucich alone with the controls. "Open up," he said, "and stand by to slap her shut in a hurry."

He stepped into the lock and stood by the open door.

It slid open part way. Barron said, "That's enough." He peered around the edge. Hlann's jeep had now outdistanced the forefront of the crowd, which was beginning to falter a bit as though realizing that it was already too close for safety if the ship should suddenly take off. Hlann was shouting at them, waving them back. He looked up and saw Barron in the lock.

"Get out of here," he shouted. "Esha is closed to Earthmen."

"Why, damn you?" Barron cried. "I was born here!" He leaned out of the lock, shouting angrily. "What do you mean, Esha is closed?"

The crowd saw him and began again a bloodthirsty howling. Pellets cracked close by his head. He pulled in, stepping behind the shelter of the door. He could still see, at an oblique angle, the silver jeep racing to turn the crowd back. And he heard Hlann's voice crying.

"—can't hold them, Sam. Take her off. The Pleiades are closed!"

LUCICH SLAMMED the lock shut. He stared at Barron. "The *Pleiades* are closed?"

"That's what he said." Barron stared at Lucich, thinking. Thinking, they can't do that, I've got a full cargo and not much else, at this stage of the game. Not enough food and fuel to go anywhere else, and no place else to go.

"I think that's what he said," said Barron, hoping that he was wrong.

Viji shook his head. "I heard him. We might as well lift."

"But *why?*" demanded Lucich. "That's what I want to know." He looked at Barron. "I thought these were such great pals of yours. Hah! They wouldn't even tell you—"

"Oh, shut up," Barron said, and went back to the bridge. The silver jeep was herding the crowd back out of harm's way. Barron strapped into the pilot's seat and punched the relay that sounded the wheezy siren.

"Stand by for take-off."

Lucich, Viji, and the three other men of *Starlady*'s crew—two mechanics and a man who would have taken a degree in electronics if he had done his studying in classrooms and not in bars—also strapped themselves into the ancient and sagging recoil chairs. Of the six, only Barron and Lucich were of Earth descent, and only Lucich came from a world outside the Pleiades.

Starlady belched, roared, and lumbered heavily into the sky, a beautiful sky of a blueness never dreamed of on Earth, flecked with mists of silver. Barron watched Esha fall away below him, the spaceport with the fringing groves of trees, the city of Khar-esh beyond it sprawling casually up and down over low hills in the bend of a river—a small city, really no more than a town of little white houses built of the river mud, cool and dim inside against the hot glare of the sun. One of the houses was his. Trees surrounded the town, cultivated groves shading out into virgin forest. The forests spread into vast blobs of blue-green and silver, dotted with other and more distant towns, pocked with flat prairies, wrinkled and humped with mountains. There was the flat glimmer of a distant sea. Then it ran all together in a blue haze, became a disc and then a round ball, and the sky was gone, and *Starlady* was out in open space.

And Esha was closed to him.

The Pleiades were closed.

He swore, bitterly, indignantly. "They can't do it," he said. "I've traded here all my life. So did my old man. My mother died on Esha, she's buried there. They can't keep me off. And what about the others?"

"What others?" growled Lucich, unconcerned with sentiment, seeing the rich worlds of the Pleiades glimmering away before his reaching hands.

"Red DeWalt," said Barron, naming them off. "Johnny Petrako. Old Man Kirk. Samelson and Collins. The bunch. They're all like us. They'll lose everything they've got if they're barred out of trade."

"So let them cry for themselves," said Lucich. "I'm worried about me."

Viji said, "Worry for all of us. Without more fuel and more supplies, we become a nice derelict somewhere in space."

Starlady had just come from one of the hub worlds at Vega, where she had picked up her cargo in a market so big it covered most of a planet. Esha was her first worldfall in the Pleiades, and Barron had counted on replenishing his supplies there. He might go on, easily enough, to any of the two thousand or more stars in the group that had inhabited planets and were within reasonable reach. But with all the ports of the Pleiades closed against him, it wouldn't be much use. *Starlady* couldn't go forward and she couldn't go back. She might as well stay where she was.

Barron flicked the controls and *Starlady* waddled her wide beam into an orbital pattern, moving slowly above Esha.

Lucich said, "What are you doing?"

"Heading for the shadow."

"Why?"

"I'm going to hang there until Khar-esh comes around. Then I'm going to take the skiff and go down there and find out what the devil goes on."

Lucich looked at him. "Who inherits the ship?" he asked sarcastically. "Not that it matters much."

"Don't be in such a hurry to count the flock before the eggs are laid," said Viji. "Sam will come back, I see to the skiff."

He went out, yelling for the mechanics.

Sam Barron took *Starlady* into the shadow and hung her there, between the dark planet and the glorious night sky of the Pleiades, with the stars burning like great lamps in the misty nebulosity that wraps them, all golden and soft and glowing.

When it was night in Khar-esh too, Barron got into the little skiff and dropped away from *Starlady*, down toward the black unwelcoming face of the world that had changed so suddenly from home to a deadly ambush.

CHAPTER TWO

BARRON LANDED in a place he knew of about four miles from the city, where a series of wide granite shelves gave the forest no roothold. There was no reason why anyone should find the skiff there before dawn, nor indeed after it. Barron left it and went off through the forest.

After an hour or so of blundering about in the warm aromatic dark, tripping on roots and getting slapped by the low-hanging feathery fronds of the honey-tree, he found the path he was looking for and went much faster, so that presently he was at the edge of the city.

Here he became infinitely cautious. He had dressed in a dark close-fitting coverall that merged his wiry middle-sized form almost indistinguishably into the shadows. His own close-cropped hair was like a dark cap on his head—an un-Eshan characteristic, but in this case good protective coloration. His face, burned to the color of saddle leather by the many suns of the Pleiades, gave off no highlights. He moved softly, clinging close to walls or the shadowing gloom under clumps of trees.

There was a queer feeling about the city. It was too quiet, too closed in behind shuttered windows. Usually people were abroad in the warm night. Usually there was a sound of voices and laughter and music. Tonight there was not a murmur.

Or was there?

Barron frowned, listening to a faint echo carried on the still air. But he could not place it. It made him uneasy. It made him realize that no matter if he had been born here, no matter if he thought of this city and this planet as home, they were not really his, nor were these people really his. It made him understand how many things there were about Esha that he did not know.

He climbed to the crest of one of the outlying hills and looked out over Khar-esh, standing guiltily under a tree at the back of somebody's garden.

The river ran wide and placid below him to the right. Above him the sky was a golden pall looped and fringed with stars, folded here and there with darkness where the nebulous clouds were split apart. In front of him was the city, darker than usual, its welcoming door-lamps unlit, its streets deserted. Only in one place was there light.

That was around the temple on the top of the highest hill. There many lamps and torches burned, so that even at this distance Barron could see the gleaming golden helix that spiraled up more than a hundred feet high. The ground and the paved court around it looked an odd color. After a minute he realized he was looking at neither ground nor paving, but a close-packed mass of people. And now he could hear more clearly the puzzling and unfamiliar echo. It was the subdued voice of a great crowd reciting solemnly together. He could not make out the words at all, but the peculiar rhythm struck hauntingly on his memory as though he had heard it before in some totally different context.

Whatever it was, it was upsetting. Apart from the amazon societies and some obscure colleges of priest-scientists, nobody bothered much with the temples. Esha was an old world. Whatever of the primitive there was about her was only the regression to simplicity of a people who had tried every manner of complication and worn them out. She had exhausted faith and scientific research at about the same time, so that these two bitter enemies had finally made peace and joined together in a desperate attempt to save themselves from oblivion. They were still alive, but that was about all.

Now, for the first time, most of the people of Khar-esh were packed into the sacred precinct of the helix, going through some solemn rite. They were angry, and afraid. Barron could hear it in their voices, feel it in the tight silence of the city. Something had happened, something deeply shocking to these normally light-hearted, indolent people.

He knew without any doubt that if they caught him they would kill him. And he began to wonder if what he had set out to do was possible.

If even his best and oldest friends, his foster-family, would still receive him.

He had a sudden overwhelming desire to run back to the skiff and take off. But he could not see what he would do after that, and so he went furtively down the other side of the hill instead.

And came within a hair's breadth of running into a party of black-clad amazons marching along toward the temple with a prisoner. Barron got a fleeting glimpse of him—an Earthman of the type that can be found on any world at all that has an oxygen atmosphere and gutters. This one had been around for a year or so. Now his hands were bound and blood ran down his face. Two of the women were holding him up. His eyes shone large and glassy in the torchlight. He looked like a man already dead.

Barron lay flat on his belly behind a wall until they were gone. Then he went on, running like a cat through dark lanes.

The house was unlighted when he came to it. Perhaps they, too, were all at the temple. He hoped not, because he would have to wait for them and every minute he stayed in Khar-esh made just that more chance of being caught. He went through the back gate and through the garden, sweet-smelling with masses of flowers pale under the glowing sky, up to the low door.

He listened for a moment with his ear against the cool plastic panel. He could hear nothing. He rapped lightly with his knuckles, but there was no answer. Exercising his rights as a foster-son, he opened the door and stepped quickly inside, closing it behind him.

THE ROOM WAS DARK. All the shutters were closed, so that not even the sky-glow filtered through. Barron spoke, and then for the first time he thought he heard a sound from somewhere deeper in the house. He went toward it.

"Shakhi?" he said. "Father?"

A tiny light sprang up, a spark close-held in the darkness of a shuttered room. It illumined the face of Shakhi, standing just beyond the doorway. An old face. Older than Barron remembered, the features made to look almost fleshless by the pinching and drawing-in of emotional strain. But the white crest was as thick and defiant as ever, the blue eyes as keen.

"Sam," he said. "I prayed you wouldn't come, but I knew you would." He drew him into the room—a sleeping room, where heavy curtains were drawn over the windows in addition to the shutters. "The others are at the temple. I pleaded sick, and stayed behind. Sam, there is bad trouble. In all my life I have not seen any like it."

Barron said, "What is it? What happened?"

Shakhi sat down, still holding the tiny flame cupped in his hands. He wore a garment of white silk and the room smelled sweet as the garden outside, and as fresh. Barron sat down on a carved stool at his side. The silence, inside the house and out, made his nerves jump and his flesh crawl. The only sound was that distant chanting.

Shakhi said, "One of the sacred women of the helix has been taken by an Earthman."

Barron stared at him. "One of the amazons? I'll admit it's surprising but—"

"No." The old man shook his head. "An amazon—" He shrugged. "Her sisters would have wished to tear her to pieces, perhaps, but it would not have set the whole world crazy. No. This woman was a full initiate—one of the Seven Keepers."

Now, for the first time, Barron began to understand, at least partly. He knew that such religion as there was on Esha centered around the so-called sacred knowledge handed down from past ages—most of it, actually, not sacred at all in nature but scientific. There was a sanctuary on a plateau far to the east, where what had anciently been a college was now The College, most hallowed spot on Esha and the home of the Seven Keepers—a batch of semi-legendary women who traditionally guarded some secret far too awesome and powerful to be trusted to any but the initiate. He had never thought much about the whole business one way or another, and he doubted if many others had either. But he could understand why the defection of one of the Sacred Seven with all her secret knowledge might upset them badly.

But not this much. Not enough to start a holy war against all Earthmen. Not enough to frighten a whole population back into its lost religion. Certainly not enough to bar shut every port in the Pleiades.

He said so.

Shakhi looked at him. He looked so grave and strange that Barron hardly knew him.

"There is more to it than you know," he said. "The Seven are not merely ritual priestesses. They do, actually and in fact, possess a very great and dreadful power. That much I know, because in the past there has been a Keeper in my own family. And now the ports of the Pleiades are shut against all Earthmen because they do not know which one Earthman may now have that power, and they do not want it loosed upon their worlds."

"What power?" asked Barron, still not believing that anything could be that frightening.

Shakhi said simply, "The power of creation. Not children, Sam. No. These women deny themselves that, to keep their minds clear of distraction. No, not children. Matter."

Barron repeated stupidly, as though he had never heard the word before, *"Matter?"*

"Matter. Out of energy, with their own minds and the help of a machine. Our people were scientists in their time, Sam. We have lost interest and forgotten, but their knowledge is as true now as it ever was. The Seven Keepers have preserved this part of it, this most dangerous and important part, against a time when we may need it for our own survival."

"I see," Barron said. "Yes, I see."

The creation of matter out of energy, by the power of a trained mind linked with or strengthened by some kind of a machine. The man who controlled a secret like that could be a god, or a demon, or the richest man in the Galaxy. Or all three.

"Who is he? The Earthman, I mean. Or does anybody know?"

"Oh, yes, they know. That is why your life is in particular danger, Sam—why even we must move carefully because you were our foster-son. It's an old friend of yours, the Earthman with the fire-colored hair. DeWalt."

"Red DeWalt?" Barron sprang up and began to stride about the room. Suddenly he was furious. "Why, damn it, I was feeling sorry for him just a little while ago, up there. So it was Red, was it? So all this is his fault. And I was the one that made him welcome here."

"He has ill repaid your hospitality," said Shakhi.

"Red DeWalt," Barron said again. And then there was silence, underlined by the sound of chanting coming distantly from the temple hill.

Barron turned and stood before Shakhi, looking down.

"Suppose I find DeWalt and this woman," he said. "Suppose I bring her back."

Shakhi nodded, over the small flame. "That is what you must do," he said, "or else you must leave the Pleiades forever."

"I'll find them," Barron said.

Shakhi blew out the flame. He stood up, his silken garment rustling softly. He said, "DeWalt will not easily give up the woman."

"He'll give her up," Barron said grimly.

"There is one other thing you should know. The woman was not taken by force, Sam. She went of her own free will."

"That," Barron admitted, "may complicate things."

"The initiates are not given much choice," Shakhi said. "The College picks them for certain powers of the mind, whether they wish it or not. Most of them consider it a high honor, but I imagine a young and lovely woman might well long for a less important but more enjoyable life. This one is young, and is said to be lovely."

Barron grunted. He started along the hall toward the back door. "I don't suppose there's any hint of where DeWalt took her."

"No. Nowhere in the Pleiades, however—that is certain. My own guess would be somewhere among the Companions."

"That would be my guess too, knowing Red. He's been there before." The Companions were an anomalous rag-tag of stars outside the Pleiades, moving in the same direction and having the same speed, but not part of the group proper. Barron had been there, too. People went to the Companions the way people on Earth long ago had gone to several well-known places, for no good.

He felt for Shakhi's hand in the dark and gripped it. Then cautiously he opened the door.

Everything was as dark and quiet as it had been. He made his way to the gate and stepped through it into the narrow back lane.

Someone came running full tilt into him from around a bend. And from somewhere not far behind him there rose a sudden clamor of female voices, sharp and cruel as the voices of wolves.

CHAPTER THREE

BARRON CAUGHT the shadowy figure in his arms and stifled its startled cry with a rough hand.

"Quiet," he whispered fiercely, and raised his fist to strike.

"Sam," said the figure, panting and wriggling in his grasp. "It's me. Ybra."

"Good Lord," said Barron, and let him go. Ybra was his foster brother, Shakhi's youngest, and younger than himself by ten years. "I thought you were at the temple."

"I sneaked away. We knew you might come tonight, and I wanted to wait with Shakhi, but they made me go— The amazons, Sam. I think they're following me. Listen..."

The female voices were howling again, closer at hand. Barron gave Ybra a desperate push toward his gate.

"Get on in. If they see you with me—"

But Ybra said, "You know what happened? Are you going to try to find DeWalt?"

"Yes. Now will you go?"

"I know where he is. I heard tonight at the temple. Everybody seems sure of it. That's why I came back. I thought if you–"

"Where, boy? *Where?*"

"One of the pleasure worlds in the Companions. The woman—"

Barron motioned him to silence. Now, quite plainly, he could hear the swift trampling of sandal-shod feet in the dust of the lane. At the same time, abruptly, there were shrill cries from the wider street at the front of the house. The amazons had split into two parties.

"No one was supposed to leave the temple until it was all over," Ybra whispered. "I thought I could get away, but the streets are crawling with the Black Ones. I don't think they know who I am."

"Good," said Barron. "This way, over the wall."

They vaulted the low wall into a neighboring garden and crouched there, hugging the shadows. Not a bare second later the amazons passed by in the lane, making hungry noises as they went. Barron shivered. The amazon societies were few and small in numbers, and in ordinary times people looked upon them with the amused scorn of the normal for the professionally queer. But they were highly trained and fanatically dedicated, and for probably the first time in their lives they were running unrestrained, holy assassins glorying in the *jihad*.

He waited until the sound of their voices had receded to what he considered a safe distance. Then he whispered to Ybra, "Go now. And thanks."

"I want to go with you, Sam. Let me?"

"What would Shakhi say to me if I got you killed?" He gave Ybra's shoulder an affectionate shake. "Go on now, quick, before they come back."

Too proud to beg, Ybra said coldly, "The woman's name is Laryl. Perhaps that will help you locate them. Good bye."

He crept past Barron to the gate and opened it silently, and then darted out into the lane.

A savage, piercing cry transfixed him. Barron leaped up and looked over the wall. The amazons, at fault, had turned and one of them had run far enough on the back track to catch sight of Ybra. Instantly the boy spun around and came rushing back. Barron caught a glimpse of his face in the sky-glow. He was scared, but he was grinning.

"You've got to take me along now, Sam," he said.

Barron did not even try to argue with him. It was obviously impossible for the boy to get home now, and it was better for them to stay together than for Ybra to be alone. From the sound of their voices, Barron judged that the amazons had lost whatever original intention they had had of mere arrest, and were now only interested in catching their prey.

Barron said, "Come on!" and ran through the garden, with Ybra close on his heels.

THEY PASSED the house, as lightless and silent as Shakhi's had been. Barron knew the family that lived here. He wondered if they were at the temple, or if they were hiding behind the shuttered windows, listening and afraid. He did not stop to find out. The amazons were in full cry now behind them. He vaulted the low front wall and crossed the wider lane, or street, and vaulted another wall there into another garden. But it was useless to continue in a straight line. He veered sharply to the right.

"North," he panted. "To the river. Maybe these harpies can't swim."

Ybra laughed silently, like a child excited by a game. He ran close to Barron, scaling the garden walls with the ease of one still fresh from orchard-raiding. Behind them in the night the amazons screamed like eagles.

The houses began to thin out. There were marshes here beside the river, unhealthy and often flooded. There was a strong wet smell of mud and pungent grasses and decay. Clumps of reed-like trees with amphibious, humped-up roots, dotted the pools and twisting waterways. Barron and Ybra fled across the marsh, splashing and floundering, and thousands of startled birds rose up out of their sleep, flapping heavily in confused and screaming clouds. The voices of the amazons were lost in the din. Once more Ybra laughed.

"The birds will help us," he said. "I think we're safe now."

Barron only grunted and ran the harder. The river water received him, startlingly cold on his overheated body. He plunged into it and swam and then lay quiet and let the current take him. Ybra floated easily beside him, on his back, so that his white crest should not make a target from the shore.

From among the wheeling clouds of birds came a scattering of sharp sounds, followed by small random explosions in the water. Then the current bore them away. It became quieter. Barron rid himself of his light boots. The water was beginning to feel warm now and its gurgling rush was pleasant. The sky overhead was still bright, wrapped in its clouds of misty light as yet unpaled by dawn. He calculated how far the river should carry them, and how long it would take to reach the space-skiff, approaching the granite ledges from the other side. He figured that they should get there before daylight.

Ybra would certainly have to come with him now, all the way. The amazons must have seen the two of them together, and even by night they would be able to identify him as an Earthman. The boy's life would not be worth a counterfeit credit if he went back now.

"I could wish," he said, "that you'd kept your valuable information to yourself."

Ybra chuckled and rolled in the water, shaking his white crest. "I've always wanted to go to space. Now I shall."

"Young whelp," said Barron, and the river took them, warm and gentle as a mother, on its curving way.

Ybra touched Barron's shoulder and pointed up. Both of them sank lower in the water. The temple hill rose above them, some distance back from the river, crowned with the great golden helix and ablaze with the shaking light of many torches. Barron could see clearly from here the packed masses of people around it, like a horde of white-crested ants, disturbed by waves of motion as heads were bowed or bodies bent in unison, swirling slowly with the unceasing rhythm of even a stationary crowd. The sound of the chanting came very strong and clear, borne across the water.

Less a chant than a solemn recitation. And suddenly now Barron remembered where he had heard phrases of that particular shape and rhythm before. He had been sent to school for three hateful years on one of Vega's many worlds, to acquire the science his father had not been able to teach him. The people on the hill were reciting mathematical formulae.

He started to laugh. And then somehow it did not seem particularly funny. Perhaps this was because he remembered the amazons.

The current swept them around the bend and the high hill was shut from view. When Barron guessed that they were opposite the ledges he swam ashore with Ybra and set off through the woods. The blue dawn caught them after all before they reached the space-skiff, and Barron was in a panic lest the amazons might have thought to search the woods, and be waiting for them. But the skiff was there just as he had left it, apparently undisturbed. He hustled Ybra aboard and took off, and did not stop to catch breath or dry himself until he was in open space and heading for *Starlady*. The Eshans had a few old ships and a handful of pilots, but he doubted whether any pursuit would be mounted.

He looked at Ybra, who was watching entranced as his world dropped away from him.

"There seems to have been a lot of gossip going around the temple last night. Did you hear anything else?"

"Like what?"

"Like what The College intends to do."

YBRA TURNED from the port, frowning. "Khar-esh is full of rumors, Sam. I've heard that a shipload of priests and amazons from The College is already heading toward the Companions. I've heard that The College has hired an outsider, a stranger, to go after DeWalt and the woman. A man from Altair, I think. I've heard that a whole fleet is to be sent out to exterminate all the Earthmen in the Pleiades. I've heard that the terrible power of the woman is going to destroy anybody who goes after her, and probably this whole part of space as well. I don't think any of these rumors are true."

"And yet," said Barron, "The College has lost something it can't afford to lose. It's bound to do something. And who knows what the woman might be able to do, with what she's got?"

Ybra ran his fingers through his thick crest, its whiteness contrasting strongly with his bronzed young skin.

"I know one thing," he said. "Whoever goes after the woman and brings her back, if it isn't you it won't matter. Earthmen will still be barred from the Pleiades. You can never come home."

And Barron knew that that was true.

"Somewhere in the Companions," he said slowly. "Well, I've got one advantage. I know Red DeWalt. I might be able to guess a little better than anyone else where exactly in the Companions he might be. I might be able to get there first."

He began to figure, not the probable whereabouts of DeWalt but the amount of fuel he had in *Starlady's* bunkers and the distance to the Companions expressed in terms of the consumption of that fuel. He thought he could just make it.

And of course he could refuel there. The Companions had obviously not joined the Pleiades boycott, any more than they had ever joined anything else. They were strictly for themselves.

"Pahlia," said Barron suddenly. "I'll lay you odds that's where he is."

Eagerly, Ybra said, "Are you sure?"

"No. How could I be sure? But he told me once that Pahlia was the only world he knew of where you could buy just about anything if you had enough money, sell just about anything if you had the merchandise, and do just about anything if you had the strength. Think a minute. Nobody would bother him there. He could take his time figuring out how he's going to use this knowledge the woman has, and then he'd be able to arrange almost any kind of a deal he wanted right there, because that's the kind of a place Pahlia is."

He might, Barron thought, just be kidding himself, but he was very sure he was right. Anyway, it gave him a place to start.

He would have been happier if he had been sure what The College was going to do. But on that he could only wait and see.

About Red DeWalt he tried just not to think at all. Red had been his friend for a lot of years, and he did not like to speculate on what their relationship was going to be like from now on. He doubted that Red had any realization at all of what he had done, or the effect it was having on others. That was one of the troubles with Red—he never took anything seriously except having fun and making money. For both reasons he was liable to take the woman Laryl very seriously indeed. And Red could be hell on wheels when he got started.

He shook his head at Ybra and sighed, "I wish you'd stayed home."

And Ybra grinned and said, "Before you're through, you may be glad I didn't."

Less than an hour later *Starlady* winked out of normal space and into overdrive, on the way to Pahlia.

CHAPTER FOUR

IT WAS A WEIRD and wonderful world, Pahlia. It circled an orange-yellow sun and by day the sky was a burnished gold, darkening to umber when storm clouds rose. By night the misty Pleiades hung in radiant clouds against the blackness. Much nearer, the famous Crystal Moon shone brighter than any star.

Day or night, it made no difference on Pahlia. Her business went on uninterrupted. Her cities rose in fantastic towers, glittering all night long with lights, or spread in rambling secluded suburbs among exotic trees. You could have what you wanted on Pahlia. All you had to do was imagine it, ask for it, and pay. In advance.

"A hell of a place," said Joe Lucich sourly, "to be broke in."

"It's just as well," Barron retorted. "We're not here for fun, remember?"

"It looks to me," said Lucich, "as though we're not here for anything. Five days now, and where's DeWalt? I thought you were so sure."

"Five days," said Barron mildly, "is not much time in which to search a whole world."

He had the old familiar impulse to clout Lucich, but he didn't. Neither did he admit that he was beginning to think they had drawn a blank. Not even to himself.

They were not looking, at this stage of the game, for a man and a woman. They were looking for a ship. There were seven starports on Pahlia. *Starlady* lounged at her dock in one of them, her bunkers comfortably full again and part of her cargo mortgaged to pay for it. Barron's assets, such as they were, were out of his reach on Esha. The remainder of the borrowed money was taking Barron, Lucich and Ybra on a tour of the other ports, checking to see if DeWalt's *Vagabond* was, or had been, in any of them.

They had one more starport to go.

Ybra was irritatingly unworried. He looked out the window of the public flier at a sparkling inland sea like a sheet of gold beneath them and said, "If he's not there, we'll go on to another world, won't we?"

"Yes," said Barron. "Sure. As long as our cargo holds out. And in the meantime, of course, somebody from The College may have found them already."

Ybra pointed suddenly through the window. "What are those?"

A cluster of shining domes rose out of the shallow sea, glittering like diamonds where the sun struck them.

"People," said Joe Lucich bitterly, "go down into those places to have a good time."

"But what do they *do* in them?"

"Music," said Lucich. "Drinks. Beautiful dames. All kinds of entertainment."

"How would you know?" Barron demanded. "You ever been there?"

"No," said Lucich. "And it don't look like I ever will."

The flier swept over a curving beach dotted with pavilions and rimmed with buildings of exotic design. Even from this height the place reeked of expense and a sort of calculated abandon that struck Barron as essentially phony. He had never cared much for these pleasure worlds, not because he was either stingy or prudish, but because they seemed to be full of people grimly determined to have the devil and all of a time, catered to by groups of hard-eyed men who supplied amusements with the cold efficiency of so many machines. Perhaps it was only because he wasn't geared to this high-powered stuff, but Barron had had better times for a lot less money in a number of places he could think of.

Several miles from the sea the flier dropped swiftly to a landing field for small craft adjacent to the starport. The passengers debarked and Barron headed toward the Port Authority building—quite different from the one on Esha, approximately five hundred times as big and five thousand times as busy. Lucich and Ybra trailed a little behind him, looking around. Barron became aware again of the demoralizing effect of Pahlia's light gravity and over-oxygenated air. The sun was hot, pleasantly so. Trees and flowering vines in the most improbable colors did some restrained rioting wherever there was room for them. It crossed his mind that this must have been a lovely world before commercialism came.

THEY ENTERED the tall white pylon of Port Authority and went into Registry. There were private landing-fields on all the pleasure worlds, owned by wealthy persons or corporations and used by such of their friends and associates as wished to come and go anonymously. These were beyond Barron's reach, but Red DeWalt didn't have those kinds of connections anyway. But if he had landed at any of the regular ports, his ship would be registered.

He fed the information into one of the robot clerks and waited while it searched its cavernous files. Registry was a large round room with no windows and only one door. The circular wall was a continuous panel, blinking erratically with many lights as relays linked the memory circuits behind it.

It took the robot a minute or two. While Barron and the others waited, a man came into the room. He was a very tall, very slim man in a close-fitting suit of dark silk that did not advertise either his world of origin or his occupation. He had a narrow high-boned face and a narrow skull with the black hair cropped short on it. His eyes were a brilliant and striking shade of topaz. They should have been warm eyes, Barron thought, like their color, but they were not. They were cold, dispassionate, and keen as steel.

They went over Barron and Lucich, flick, flick, seeing everything, and passing on. They flicked over Ybra, brightened suddenly with almost startled interest, looked again at the boy's white crest, flicked back to Barron and Lucich for a second glance, and then were quickly veiled. The man walked to another of the robot clerks and began unhurriedly to punch keys.

For no reason at all, Barron's hair bristled at the back of his neck. He found himself standing tense and poised as one in the presence of an enemy.

Neither Lucich nor Ybra apparently had noticed anything about the man. They were waiting for the robot to answer.

It did. *Vagabond*, Merope, Harley DeWalt owner and master, was registered and still docked.

Ybra gave a cry, "He is here, then!"

"Yeah," said Barron, and ripped the sheet out of the slot. "Let's go."

"What's wrong with you?" asked Lucich. "Isn't that what you wanted?"

"Sure," said Barron, and glared at both Lucich and Ybra. "Let's go."

He strode out the door. The tall slim man remained at his place, not looking around, as though indifferent to what they did.

Outside, Barron explained.

"He recognized you for an Eshan, Ybra. The crest of a male Eshan is unmistakable. And it gave him a definite reaction. Now why should that be?"

"I don't know, I've never seen the man before, so it couldn't be—"

"Didn't you tell me," Barron said, "that there was a rumor around that The College had hired a man to come after DeWalt?"

"Yes, there was. A man from Altair."

"Joe," said Barron to Lucich, "you've been to Altair. Did he look like anybody on those worlds?"

Lucich thought about it. "There's a lot of bean-pole types there, all right. I think they come from the fourth planet. But I don't know, Sam. I didn't look too close at this guy."

"Look again," said Ybra quietly. "There he comes out of the building."

The tall slim man emerged into the sunlight and walked without hesitation in the opposite direction. He did not so much as glance at them.

"Could be," Lucich said, and shrugged. "But there's a lot of tall skinny guys in the galaxy, you know, and they don't all come from Altair."

"I think," said Barron, "that this one did, and I think he's a professional killer. And I think we'd better polish up our luck and find DeWalt in a hurry."

"Well," said Lucich, "where do we go from here?"

Barron scowled at the sheet the robot had given him. "To the dock and have a look around—there's just a chance Red may be living aboard *Vagabond*. He's done that before, on the grounds that a man's a fool to waste money on a place to sleep, and around here even the cots have diamond-studded headboards. If he's not there, we'll start at the hotels."

He looked once again after the tall slim man, but he was out of sight now and it was impossible to tell which way he had gone.

THEY WENT BACK into the Port Authority building and took the lift down to the subway rotunda.

Here they were not alone. Crowds of people from all over this sector of space pushed and laughed and chattered—some of them just coming in, others about to leave and escorted by groups of friends, a certain number of them going to and from the ships on which they were living. Men and women of every size, shape and color, a bright kaleidoscope of gaudy silks and fluttering draperies, bare flesh, glittering teeth, glassy eyes, ornaments. Everybody joyous, everybody having fun. Ybra stared, his own eyes shining with excitement. Lucich stared too, mostly at the women.

Checking the code number of the dock, Barron found the trunk tube they wanted and stepped onto the swiftly moving walkway. The tubes ran deep under the landing-field, but even down here you could feel the shock and hear the dim thunder as some starship landed or took off.

From the main trunk smaller tubes branched off, serving the individual rows of docks. The segment of crowd that had accompanied them thinned out as the branch tubes bled them off. The sound of laughter and bright talk dwindled and finally died. Twenty people, looking jaded and worn in the harsh light, became sixteen and then seven and then four, and finally the last group vanished, still quarreling mildly over where they would go for the night's entertainment.

When Barron and the others switched onto a branch themselves, they were quite alone.

The mechanism of the walkway throbbed and whispered faintly in the enclosed space. Barron kept thinking it sounded like footsteps. He kept looking back down the tunnel, but he didn't see anyone. The lighted landings passed by at regular intervals, numbered like the docks. The landings ran clear through to the inbound tunnel and sometimes there were people on the far side getting on the walkway, heading for the gilded palaces of sin beside the inland sea. Bursts of talk and laughter came and were quickly lost again. Still Barron kept glancing uneasily back. And still he could not see anyone behind them.

"You make me nervous," Lucich said.

"Good," said Barron. "Maybe it'll help you keep your mind on your work."

They passed the landing next to *Vagabond*'s. It was empty. But for the first time Barron noticed that there was a place behind the lift-shaft that you couldn't see. There was no reason why that should have bothered him. It did.

Vagabond's landing showed ahead, a brightly lighted square of white concrete.

Barron stepped out on it. And as he did so, something moved. Something swiftly completing the act of disappearing into that very blind spot behind the lift-shaft that Barron had noticed before.

He sprang toward it, rushing over the concrete. He flung himself around the curve of the shaft and onto the person who stood there. At the last second when it was far too late to stop, it occurred to him that if the person was the tall killer from Altair this was not a very bright thing to do. He reached out his hands and caught the person by the arms, and it was not the tall killer from Altair.

It was a woman, a young woman. Very young. Tall, but no taller than a woman should be, which was to say just tall enough to give her curves plenty of room to be full without crowding. She wore a shimmering concoction of jade-green tissue that did not quite hide all the pearly lustre of the flesh it covered. Her eyes were blue and wide and frightened.

And her hair was red.

The hair of the runaway Eshan Keeper should have been snow-colored like Ybra's, long and soft instead of crested, but still white.

Barron, considerably confused, heard Lucich and Ybra running up behind him. He looked at the girl, who could not have come from anywhere but *Vagabond*, and she looked up at him, tense as a drawn bow between his hands.

"Who are you?" he asked.

In a small flat voice she answered, "I am Laura DeWalt. Harley DeWalt's sister."

Suddenly all the confusion was gone and Barron began to laugh.

"Red DeWalt never had a sister," he said. "And of course your hair isn't white, you've dyed it."

His hands tightened a little on her round arms.

"Your name is Laryl."

CHAPTER FIVE

THE WALKWAYS, one on either side of them, drummed and hummed. Barron could feel Ybra and Lucich breathing down the back of his neck, and Lucich said,

"Is *that* her?"

The girl's face was now pale and stiff with panic.

"Let go of me," she said. "I don't know you. You haven't any right to—"

She began to struggle against him. Then for the first time, looking past him, she saw Ybra. For one moment she stopped absolutely still and Barron could feel her heart pounding. Then she cried out something that sounded like, "No, no!" and lunged so quickly that she slipped out of his grasp. She ran like a deer across the platform and onto the inbound walkway.

Barron shouted after her, to wait. He ran to the walkway. But she was already some little distance away from him, carried by the swift-moving belt. She turned to look back at him, her eyes blazing, her red lips pulled back to show the edges of her teeth.

She screamed at him in Eshan, "I won't go back. You can't make me. Nobody can make me!"

She whirled around and ran, adding her speed to the moving walk, her hair and the thin green stuff of her gown flying behind her.

Barron ran, too. The tunnel was empty for the moment as far as he could see ahead, but people might come into it at any time, and he wanted to catch up with Laryl before that happened. Even on Pahlia the sight of three men subduing a screaming girl would attract attention. Lucich and Ybra ran with him. Ybra had not said anything. Apparently he was caught speechless between awe and surprise. But Lucich was never speechless.

"I don't blame her," he said. "What a crime to waste all that in a place where there's nothing but a bunch of women and dried-up priests."

Ybra finally found his tongue. "I didn't know the Keepers ever looked like that."

"I guess they're not picked for anything but their minds," Barron said, and realized all of a sudden what a terrible and awesome power this beautiful soft-fleshed girl possessed.

It turned him cold all over and made him falter in his stride. Suppose she turned it on them? She could destroy anything with it, men, planets, stars, anything.

Then he remembered that Shakhi had said that the mind required the help of some kind of a machine. Perhaps the Keepers were powerless without the machines. Certainly the girl did not seem to have thought of anything but flight.

There was something else, too. She did not fit the picture he had had of her at all. Shakhi had described her as young and lovely and so he had thought of her that way, but also he had thought of her as proud and austere and frighteningly brilliant, vested with the authority of a superhuman power. This girl wasn't any of those things.

She had wonderful legs, though. And the motion of her running was something to watch.

The next landing swept toward them. The girl was no more than twenty feet away. Barron figured that he would catch her easily in the next couple of minutes.

A man appeared on the landing.

A tall slim man in a dark suit. He stepped off onto the moving walk just ahead of Laryl.

Laryl cried out, "Help me, please help me, those men—"

He reached out one long arm and threw it around her in a gesture that was intended to appear protective. With the other he produced a gun. Barron and the others stopped running.

"When you reach the landing," the man said, in a soft and pleasant voice, "step onto it. And stay there until we are out of sight."

The belt thrummed, whisking them nearer and nearer to the landing. Barron looked at the tall man. It was obvious now that he had followed them, hiding here on the next landing to see what they would do. And Laryl had dropped right into his hands.

Barron said quietly, to Ybra and Lucich, "There's no need to get off. He isn't going to shoot us."

"How do you know," Lucich demanded, and the man from Altair echoed, smiling.

"Yes. How can you be so sure?"

"Because none of us is the man you came for, and the excitement aroused by three bodies might impede you from getting at him." His glance moved to Laryl, panting in the circle of the man's long arm. "There is also the girl."

"Yes," said the man, and nodded. "I admire intelligence. I hope yours is great enough to take you away from Pahlia— in fact, from the whole Pleiades."

THE THING HAPPENED then that Barron had been sure would happen at any minute. A group of people came out onto the landing beyond the one they had just passed. Instantly the tall man let his gun slip out of sight. He began to walk away from Barron and the others, holding the girl gently by the elbow. Over his shoulder he said,

"I might remind *you* that the bosses here rather frown on disturbances. They don't like anything that upsets the paying guests." Then he bent his head and spoke to Laryl and smiled, and she smiled, and they hurried on together. The group of people on the platform, perhaps a dozen of them, began to step off onto the walkway. Laryl and the tall man became mixed with them. By the time Barron had caught up the whole dozen were between him and the couple. He thought he could see the Altairan's head towering beyond them and he pushed and shoved his way between the people, slim bluish sprites from one of Alcyone's worlds who reproached him shrilly for his bad manners. Lucich and the boy came doggedly behind him.

When he had managed to get through the group he saw the flutter of Laryl's green gown far ahead, and then lost it as other people intervened. He did his best to catch up to it, and just before the branch joined the main trunk he did see it again. After that it was hopeless. There were too many people. But he kept working his way forward as fast as he could, stolidly ignoring the wrath he aroused in the folk he jostled.

"If we can pick them up again in the main terminal we're all right," he said. "Otherwise we might as well buy a wreath for DeWalt and go away."

"Why didn't you tell her the man was after her and DeWalt?" said Lucich. "She might of not been so easy for him to handle."

"Suppose I told her," Barron said. "Either she wouldn't believe me, or if she did, he'd have shot us and gotten her away, figuring he could always get DeWalt later. She's the most important part of the deal, you know. This way I hoped he'd figure to lose us and let her take him right to DeWalt."

"It looks like what he's doing, all right."

"What if we can't find them again at the terminal?" asked Ybra unhappily. "I don't care about DeWalt. All this is his fault, anyway. But the woman—"

"If we lose we lose," said Barron curtly. "Come on."

Laughter, chattering voices, movement, color. Faces of every shade from ebon and plump-purple to ash-white and silver, turning to glare at him. The tops of heads, the backs of them, necks, breasts, chests, arms, shoulders, bodies thick and thin, short and tall. The smell of different peoples like a blend of spices, piquant and a little overpowering. Barron was glad when they reached the terminal. It seemed to him that he had spent years struggling in a sticky river of galactic humanity.

"There she is," cried Ybra. "See? Just getting into the lift there."

A flutter of green, a glint of red hair. Then the door closed. Barron put his shoulder down and butted through the crowd, with Lucich and Ybra at his sides forming a wedge. They forced their way into another lift. When it reached ground level Laryl and the man from Altair were already out of sight. Barron ran across the lobby and through the broad exit into the glare of the setting sun outside.

Laryl and the Altairan were getting into a 'copter-cab some fifty feet away. Their backs were turned. Barron retreated quickly into the shadow of the exit, motioning Lucich and the boy to stay out of sight. He watched the cab lift off, and he could see the pale blur of the Altairan's face behind the window as he looked back to see whether Barron had followed them. The cab was bright blue with silver markings. It rose up, hovered a moment while the Altairan apparently took a good long look, and then veered away toward the city.

A vast sense of relief came over Barron. The man was going after DeWalt, making the girl help him. He had been afraid that he might think better of it and make sure of the girl by taking her back to Esha at once.

Ybra was tugging at him impatiently. "If you don't hurry there won't be a cab left. Look at that mob."

"We're not taking a cab. He's not that careless. He'll take some pains to make sure he isn't being followed, and I want him to be certain he's lost us." Barron pointed to the terminus of the high-speed elevated tube that connected the spaceport with the city. The top and sides of the tube were of glassite, so that the passengers might enjoy the superb view. "We'll ride that. We ought to be able to keep him in sight."

No easy task. But not impossible. Cab and tube both went in the same direction and at about the same rate of speed.

The blue cab was now far enough away for figures on the ground to be unrecognizable from it. Barron moved fast, heading for the tube.

There was no jostling, no running ahead on this express belt. Padded rests caught and held the passenger in pneumatic comfort and safety while the belt rushed smoothly forward. The transparent curve of the tube showed the spaceport on one side, huge and impressive with its rows of towering starships all catching the sunset on one side. From the landing field farther out a tender-crane as big as an apartment house was trundling a pleasure craft toward its assigned dock. On the other side were trees and pleasant villas, and in the distance the golden sea flashing like hot metal.

In the sky above was a blue cab with silver markings. There were other cabs too, all moving in a stream toward the city. But with three of them to watch, it proved not too difficult to keep the right one in sight.

Until they reached the city. Then they left it behind, slowed by increasingly heavy traffic while the tube-belt rushed on unimpeded.

They got off the belt at the first platform. Here they were on the edge of the inland sea, with the pale beaches stretching in both directions. Far out in the bright water the pleasure domes flashed in the eye of the sinking sun.

Desperately Barron scanned the sky above for the blue cab. If they lost it now probably both DeWalt and the girl would be lost, and the Pleiades would be closed to him forever.

He watched, and it came, drumming down out of the sky as though it knew what was decreed for it. It dropped onto a landing-field from whence the boats left for the pleasure domes. From where he stood on the high platform Barron could see the small figures of Laryl and the man from Altair get out of the cab and enter a boat.

"That's where DeWalt is," Barron said. "In the domes. Good. Let's go."

He turned toward the lift shaft. And two men were there. They had got off the belt and had stood quietly admiring the view for a minute or two. Barron had hardly noticed them in his intentness on the cab. Now they stood between him and the lift and one of them said.

"Arrikon dislikes very much to be followed. That is our whole business in life—to see that no one follows him."

He smiled, a kind of mechanical movement of the lips with no humor in it. His companion did not even do that. And each one carried in his hand a needle-gun, a squat little instrument practically unnoticeable to anyone passing by, but as deadly as a cannon at short range if the steel projectiles hit a vital spot.

"Well," said Barron mildly, "in that case I guess we'll have to change our plans. Come on, boys."

He turned halfway around as though he was going to go back to the tube again, bent suddenly at the knees and flung himself low at the two men.

CHAPTER SIX

THEY WERE STANDING close together, so that the impact of his body staggered them both off balance. They were brought to face each other and so were momentarily afraid to shoot. Barron grabbed one around the hips and used him as a lever, kicking furiously at the other man.

He felt his boot sink deep into yielding flesh. There was a deep hollow gasping noise. Then Lucich and Ybra were on top of them. The man he was holding cursed and lost his footing, falling back against the smooth wall of the lift-shaft.

Barron fell with him. The needle-gun went *whick-whick-whick* close to his ear. He squirmed around and got his hands on the man's wrist. He pushed the gun up and twisted. Ybra was hitting the man around the head, strong awkward blows. The man was in a black rage. He kneed and kicked and floundered, beating Barron on the face with his free hand.

Barron tasted blood and there was now something wrong with his left shoulder. A thin hot wire had been strung through it, and his whole arm was weak. Still he hung on, twisting at the gun.

The man got his back against the smooth wall and braced his feet and lunged upward. He gave Ybra the point of his elbow in the throat, knocking him out of the way. Then he began to hammer Barron across the back of the neck with the hard edge of his hand. Barron pulled his head down between his shoulders. He braced his own feet and butted. He drove the man back hard against the wall. He was angry. He was hurt and bloody and full of hate. He wanted to kill this man, and the other man, and Arrikon. After that, he wanted to kill Red DeWalt.

He butted. He had a broad hard head and he used it. He used his knees and feet. The man was not fighting so much now. Barron kept beating him against the smooth wall and presently he dropped the gun. Then Barron let go of his wrist and hit him clean blows with his fists. On the fourth one the man crumpled down and was quiet.

Barron stood back, breathing hard.

Lucich was sitting on the other man, who had been easy prey for him after Barron's kick in the belly. Barron glowered at Lucich.

"What the hell are you just sitting there for?" he demanded. "Why didn't you help?" He put his hand up to his shoulder, where a needle had gone through the muscle.

Lucich got up. "I'm saving myself," he said. "I'm probably going to want to run real fast before I'm through."

Barron grunted. Ybra was leaning against the wall with his hands on his bruised throat, and his mouth open. His eyes looked surprised and shocked. Barron said, "I told you to stay at home. Come on."

He helped the boy into the lift. Lucich stopped to pick up the gun of the man Barron had knocked out. He already had the other. Then he got into the lift too. They went down.

In the shadow of a clump of flowering trees they paused to clean up, using water from an ornamental pool. Lucich did the best he could with Barron's shoulder, which had already stopped bleeding and was now merely increasingly painful. The needles did not make a big hole, but you knew it all right when one went through you. Ybra had got his breath again but his voice was hoarse and now he looked mad, too, as mad as Barron felt. Barron grinned. He took one of the needle-guns from Lucich. Then they went to the shore and took a boat out to the domes.

It was full dark now and the wind over the water was cool. The Crystal Moon—Pahlia had no natural satellites—hung huge and brilliant in the sky.

Ybra looked up at it. "What do people do up there?"

"Same things they do in the domes," said Lucich. "Only it's fancier—no gravity, and all that."

Entry into the domes cost them a considerable part of what they had left in the way of money. From the upper lock they went down to the gallery that circled each one of the interconnecting domes. It was early but already the gallery and the floors below were crowded with people eating and drinking, gambling or watching the gambling. The domes were lighted from the outside, very cleverly, so that those within had the feeling of being genuinely under water. The gaming tanks were lighted, brightly, but otherwise the illumination was wavering and subdued so that people seemed to float in it. Various creatures of the sea, beautiful, grotesque, dark or vividly colored, hung around the domes and peered in curiously at the people, their eyes shining in the light.

Barron began to hunt for Red DeWalt.

THERE WAS NO SIGN of him, nor of Laryl and Arrikon, in the first of the domes, which was devoted to food and liquor. Knowing Red, Barron hurried on to where the gaming tanks were.

In a broad shallow tank equipped with jets a number of small crustaceans, colored red and green and black, were demonstrating the theory of random distribution on a glass bottom marked off like a graph. A lot of people hung over the tank railing making bets, but Red was not one of them.

In the third and largest dorm there was a tank the size of a large swimming pool. In it some beautiful but slightly repellent amphibian girls and some vaguely humanoid sea-things were doing something in the way of a competitive game. This seemed to be very popular. Red was not here, either.

The fourth dome was darker than the others. The illumination had a reddish tinge. The tank here was deeper and had a protective network of steel bars over it against the possibility of some drunk falling in. The crowd around it was almost entirely male. In the starkly brilliant waters of the tank two lean jut-jawed fish as big as bulldogs, color-banded for easy identification, tore at each other with blind ferocity, surrounded by lacy patterns of drifting blood.

But not in this dome, either, was Red DeWalt to be found.

The fifth dome was closed. Curtains of metallic cloth hung over the entrance and a velvet-covered chain crossed it. A sign begged the indulgence of the customers while the dome was being renovated and redesigned for their great enjoyment in the future.

The battle in the tank was reaching its climax. The bettors seemed more excited than the fish, which were killing each other. No one was paying any attention to Barron. He said quietly to Ybra, "You stay out here." He nodded to Lucich and took the needle-gun into his fist. Then he stepped over the velvet-covered chain and slid quickly between the curtains.

The dome beyond was not lighted, except by reflection from the other domes. Through its walls the sea floor was visible, set with waving clumps of reed in which dim creatures moved. There were all the signs of work on progress, dropped now and waiting for morning. The tank in the center was dry.

The girl Laryl sat on the floor amid a heap of unnamed objects gathered together and covered with protective cloths. Her attitude was curiously like that of a rag doll, limp and sprawled. She was watching, with no particular interest, the efforts of the man from Altair to break Red DeWalt's back over the railing of the tank.

Barron went forward in swift leaping strides.

Arrikon heard him and turned his head. In the faint light his eyes appeared filmed and pale, part of the pale intensity of his face. His long thin body was arched, his legs locked over DeWalt's thighs, his long thin arms held straight under the hammer curve of his shoulders, his hands around DeWalt's neck, pushing. DeWalt was a strong man. He was not nearly as tall as Arrikon but he was thick and heavy-muscled. He did not break easily. But he was closer to it than Barron would have thought possible.

"Let him up," Barron said.

Arrikon regarded him from some strange inner distance and did not move.

"I have a needle-gun," Barron said, and held it out so that Arrikon could see it. "I took it away from your strong-arm man. I will give you one second to let go. After that I will shoot you in the spine."

Arrikon closed his eyes like a bird of prey and opened them again, and now the filmy look was gone and they were cold and cruel and alert. He took his hands away from DeWalt's neck and stepped aside. DeWalt slid heavily off the rail and down to the floor where he sat with his head against the railing and his chest heaving with a noise like sobbing. For the first time Barron noticed a knife on the floor near Arrikon's feet. DeWalt's collar was stained with blood below and behind the right ear. Arrikon had apparently slugged DeWalt preparatory to a quiet stabbing, but had underestimated the hardness of DeWalt's skull.

Barron showed his teeth. "This hasn't exactly been your night, has it?" he said to Arrikon. He nodded toward the girl, who was still staring vaguely with idiot eyes. "What did you do, drug her?"

"It was advisable." Arrikon wiped the palms of his hands across his silk tunic and then let them rest on his hips, DeWalt, blowing like a whale, was trying to get his feet under him.

"Help him," Barron said to Lucich. "Out of the way. That's it. Now get some of that cordage there and tie this gentleman up. Tight."

He moved in a little closer. "From here I can shoot you in the face, I wouldn't try anything."

Arrikon shrugged. He put his hands behind him and let Lucich tie them.

"It's a long way to Esha," he said. "In fact, it's a long way just from here to your ships. Longer than you know. I can wait."

Lucich tied him to the rail and shoved a gag in his mouth. "That'll hold him for a while," he said. Barron nodded. He turned to DeWalt, who was now standing up and moving his head carefully back and forth. Barron reached out and got hold of the front of DeWalt's tunic and looked darkly into his face.

"I ought to finish what he started," Barron said. "Right here and now."

"What the devil for?" DeWalt said, staring at him. "What did I do? I wish somebody would tell me what's going on. First this so-and-so, and now you."

"You don't know?" Barron said. He pointed to the, girl. "I don't suppose you know who she is, then."

"Her?" said DeWalt. "Sure. Those old creeps on Esha had her shut up in The College, but she didn't want to be a priestess so I took her with me. So what?"

Now it was Barron's turn to stare. "Didn't you know she was one of the Keepers?"

"Look," said DeWalt. "Here comes this cute chick, about the cutest I ever saw, and tells me she's where she hates it and she wants to go away with me. Do I argue? Do I ask her a lot of questions? Do I worry whether the Great High Mumbo Jumbo likes it or not? Would you?"

He shook Barron's hands away. "The hell with you, I need a drink."

"Wait a minute," said Barron. "Wait just a minute. Then you don't know why she's so important? Why The College hired this man to kill you because she's talked to you? Why every port in the Pleiades is closed to Earthmen because of her?"

"Every port is *what?*" said DeWalt.

"Closed. Shut. Barred. You can't go back. I can't go back. None of us can, because of you and your cute chick."

DeWalt shook his head. "You're kidding. Sam, this isn't any time for that. I've just almost been killed. I need a drink."

Barron began to laugh. He stopped it, looking at Arrikon's yellow eyes, alert and brilliant above the gag. "Let's go," he said to DeWalt. "I'll explain to you somewhere else."

Now DeWalt looked at Arrikon. "Next time," he said, "I'll know better than to turn my back on you." He bent over Laryl. He started to help her up and almost fell on her instead. "Drugged, huh? And he told me she was sick. That's how he got me here."

BARRON PUSHED him aside. He and Lucich took the girl between them and stood her up and began to walk her toward the door. DeWalt followed unsteadily, Arrikon remained motionless. Barron had a strong impulse to go back and kill him as a simple matter of safety, but he could not force himself to cold-blooded murder.

They rejoined Ybra and made their way back through the domes. Nobody paid much attention to them. In the first dome DeWalt stopped at the bar and ordered a drink. Then he nodded toward Laryl, standing limp and vacant between the two men.

"One of your best snapper-outers," DeWalt said to the bartender. "She's had a bit too much of a time."

The bartender smiled, nodded, and produced a capsule and a small glass of pink liquid. "Give the lady this," he said, "and she'll dance all night."

While they were getting the stuff down Laryl's throat the two men they had fought with on the tube-platform entered the dome. Both of them looked the worse for wear. They saw Barron and his party and glared with the most vicious hostility, but that was all they did. Barron nodded to them and then got Laryl and DeWalt moving toward the port. He saw the two men move off through the domes, obviously looking for Arrikon.

It was only a question of a little time before they would find him. A sudden fever to get away, not only from the domes but from Pahlia itself, came over Barron. He hustled them all into a boat and was relieved when it pulled away from the landing.

"She's coming out of it," DeWalt said, holding Laryl's head so the cool wind would blow in her face.

"Look at her. Pretty as they make 'em. I wouldn't say she's weighed down any with brains, but with what else she's got she don't need 'em."

"No," said Barron, thinking of something DeWalt was not thinking about, "apparently she doesn't. Listen, Red. We'll go back to your *Vagabond* and I'll radio Viji to bring *Starlady* here. I've got to take this girl back to Esha myself, and I'd advise you to stay away from there. I—"

Laryl sneezed violently three times in quick succession, and then she said, "Esha? No. No, no!"

"Now, then," DeWalt said, patting her. "Take it easy, kid." He looked at Barron. "That's a devil of a thing to do,

Sam. She doesn't want to go back and I sure don't want her to either. I don't see—"

"Listen," said Barron. "Do you want to go on living in the Pleiades? Do you want to go on trading there? Then she's got to go back. You committed about the biggest sacrilege you could and—"

Laryl stood up. She turned around and began to strike at Barron with her hands, crying hysterically, "I won't go back, I won't!"

Barron ducked to avoid a raking blow to the eye and Laryl overbalanced. The boat's side caught her at the knees. She toppled over towards the flying spray, and screamed as she went.

Ybra caught her. For a moment the two of them hung on dead center, her weight against his braced strength. Then slowly he pulled her in. She collapsed onto the seat beside him and he said to Barron, shakily,

"I told you you'd be glad I came."

Laryl began to cry. She beat her hands up and down on her bare white knees and wailed. "Why does everything have to be against me? I just want to live a little and have fun. I don't want to be anybody important." Barron touched her shoulder and she yelled at him, "I'll die if I have to go back!"

"All right," said Barron soothingly, "we'll talk about it later. Maybe we can find some other way out. But the important thing now is to get away before Arrikon makes another try. You don't want Red to get killed, do you?"

Her eyes were wide and wet and dismal. "Arrikon? Who's that?"

"The tall man. The man who tried to kill Red back there in the dome."

"It was all fuzzy," she said. "I don't remember much. I thought he was helping me. Why does he want to kill Red?"

Barron explained, and she listened and then shrugged. "I don't see what difference it makes to me who takes me back to Esha."

"I've got an idea," Barron told her, "that Arrikon was planning to take you to a place a lot worse for you than Esha. And anyway, it makes a difference to me. If I bring you back, Earthmen are vindicated and we can go on living and trading in the Pleiades. If not, we'll starve."

She muttered that she did not care who starved, and subsided into a deep sulk. She remained that way, saying nothing, sniffling now and then, her tear-swollen eyes half shut and brooding, all the way back to the spaceport and *Vagabond*. They locked her in her cabin. Barron searched it first to make sure she did not have any weapon or any peculiar machine in it, but when he did finally leave her he did not feel easy about it. There was something ominous about her heavy silence. He didn't see what she could do, but just the thought of the power she could wield if she got the chance and wanted to, sent the cold chills up and down his back.

He radioed Viji and told him to bring *Starlady* as soon as he could, which Viji said would be as soon as he could get a tender-crane and clearance on the field for take-off—in other words, not very soon. Then he took DeWalt into the captain's cabin and sat him down over a bottle and began carefully to explain what Laryl was and why she had to go back.

DeWalt's face became a thing of wonder. The space-burn faded to a greenish gray and the freckles that had been hidden by it stood out like the spots on a star-map.

"You mean I've been travelling around with—" he said, and could not go any farther. He picked up the bottle and drank hastily. Then he put it down and said, "Take her back, friend. She's all yours."

He got up and began to pace up and down the cabin, shaking his head. "My gosh. If I'd known that I wouldn't have touched her. No wonder they've flipped all over the Pleiades. Do you suppose this Arrikon knows what she's got?"

"For sure. They wouldn't tell him at The College when they hired him, but he knows. And he wouldn't take her back to Esha, not if they gave him the whole planet. He's not the type that gets scared at the idea of power."

DeWalt moved his shoulders uneasily. "It's just not my game. I don't mind turning a dirty dollar now and then, but this is just too big. And she's such a dope, too. Honest, Sam, it's hard to believe she could really do anything like that. Are you sure the priests aren't maybe stretching the truth a little?"

Vagabond quivered suddenly, shifting a bit as though her center of balance had been somehow disturbed. Barron and DeWalt froze, startled. And then from the well of the ship there came to them Ybra's voice raised in a wild cry of alarm.

CHAPTER SEVEN

BARRON RUSHED into the well. Ybra was standing on the opposite side of the narrow catwalk that circled it, staring up. He babbled something to Barron and pointed.

Barron looked up. The well ran from stern to nose of the ship, giving access to all sections in any position. In this position the stern fins were on the ground and the nose was pointed vertically skyward. And a strange vertigo came over Barron, a queasy twisting of the innards that made him grab at the railing for support.

He was looking at the sky. The well went up so far in a normal manner and then it simply stopped and everything around it stopped---storerooms, bulkheads, holds, hull. There was nothing. Just sky.

DeWalt, beside him, made a sound of anguish and dismay. And another section of the ship began, even as they watched it, to crumble and fall away.

It fell in clouds of fine dust that blew away on the night wind or sifted down through the well to land gently on their upturned faces. It was all done quietly. Everything disintegrated at once, block by block, so that there was nothing to crash or shatter. On the catwalk above them one of DeWalt's crewmen came out to see what the trouble was. He took one look and then flung himself down the ladder. He did not stop or speak. Distantly, Barron noticed the man's face as he went by. It was stony white, the eyes and the mouth stretched wide.

"What is it?" whispered DeWalt. "What's happening?"

The dust came down, iron and steel and alloy, plastic and cloth, supplies of all kinds, the flesh and bones of a ship. Matter, dissolved and pulled apart.

Matter.

And if you can make it, you can unmake it.

But of course.

"Give me the key," said Barron. "The key to her cabin."

He had to grab DeWalt and shake him, before DeWalt gave him the key. Barron ran fast around the catwalk. Lucich had come from somewhere below. He saw him and heard him speak but Lucich was not important and he paid no attention. He unlocked the cabin door very carefully, very silently. Big drops of cold sweat ran down his face. He opened the door a crack and looked in.

Laryl was sitting cross-legged on the floor. Her face was puckered in an expression of intense preoccupation, her eyes almost shut, the tip of her pink tongue sticking out between her teeth. In her hands she held the insulated parts of two loops of wire. Between the loops was a curious crude helix, also made of wire—she must have stripped part of the cabin's light-circuit, and they had taught her enough at The College so that she could do that without electrocuting herself. She was holding the helix in a certain way and it was glowing hotly, apparently drawing power from the ship's huge batteries to augment whatever weird power of the mind Laryl had. During the second or two that Barron watched her she rotated slightly on her bottom, shifting the focus of the helix, and he knew that when she had completed a full circle another section of the ship would be gone.

Barron set his jaw hard and made a great clumsy leap ending in a kick that sent the helix flying out of her hands to lie sputtering in a corner.

It only sputtered for a second. Then it began rapidly to cool off, and Barron realized that it had not in the least been getting power from the ship's batteries nor from anywhere else but out of Laryl's disheveled head. It was not connected to anything. It was merely a focusing device. Probably anything would do as well, if Laryl only knew it. Probably that was a safety-check on the infinite psychokinetic potentialities of the Keepers, the conditioned belief that their power would only function through a helical coil. For the first time he could remember, Barron felt a strong inclination to faint from sheer unmanly fright.

Instead, translating fright into anger, he grasped Laryl and set her roughly on her feet and shook her.

"What do you think you're doing?" he shouted at her.

She laughed, sticking out her lip defiantly. "I'm ruining the ship, that's what I'm doing. Now how are you going to take me back to Esha?"

"Oh Lord," said Barron. "Why couldn't you have had brains, too?" DeWalt and Lucich were peering in through the door. He nodded to the wire helix. "Pick that thing up and get it out of here. Go ahead, it's harmless without her, and vice versa."

It was Lucich who went over and got it. DeWalt was in a daze. "She wrecked my ship," he kept saying. "My ship!" And then he said, "I'll kill her."

It took Lucich and Ybra both to hold him back.

"All right," said Barron savagely to Laryl. "Now you've advertised your power to the world, suppose we just let Arrikon have you."

"I'll do the same for him," said Laryl. "I told you, I won't let anybody take me back."

BARRON SHOOK HIS HEAD. "He won't take you back, not now. Not after you've demonstrated what you can do. Listen." Already sounds were filtering in from outside, the sounds of a crowd gathering. "No," said Barron, "you can go and be free as a bird with Arrikon. Or as free as he'll let you be, while he uses your power to set himself up as the biggest man in the galaxy."

Barron thought he knew men well enough to be pretty sure that was about what the Altairan would try to do. He was trying to produce an effect in Laryl, and he got it. Her face now lost its stubborn rigidity and became doubtful.

"Would he do that? Would he really dare—"

"He's an adventurer, a killer for profit. I doubt if his great moral sense would stop him."

"But that isn't right," Laryl said, looking as outraged as by a blasphemy. "That's the first thing they taught us at The College—that the power must never be used for gain or—"

She stopped rather suddenly. Barron said, "Or what?"

"Or for our own advantage," she said in a small voice. "Like I just did." She sat down on the bunk and put her head in her hands. "It isn't fair. I didn't want this power. I just— had it. But if they hadn't come and tested me and trained me up I wouldn't have known I had it or been able to use it, and why couldn't they just have let me alone?"

Yes, thought Barron, why indeed? The noises of the crowd were growing louder by the second, and now from the distance another one was added, a shrill insistent hooting that had an official sound to it. Barron hauled Laryl to her feet and hustled her out of the cabin, shoving DeWalt ahead of him.

"We better get out of here to the landing field, fast," he said. "And hope Viji gets *Starlady* here before it's too late."

They began to climb down the ladder. Barron looked up once at the open sky above where the encircling body of the ship ended so abruptly. He did not look at it again.

They came to the lock hatch. And it was already too late.

Motioning Ybra and Lucich to keep the girl back out of sight, Barron stepped out of the lock with DeWalt. The dock area blazed with light as it always did at night. Normally surface traffic was limited to fueling and maintenance crews and the various machines they operated. But now around DeWalt's ruined ship people had gathered and were still gathering, from other ships, from everywhere, as word spread of the incredible thing that had happened to *Vagabond*.

The crowd alone would not, perhaps, have stopped them. But the shrill hooting noise was close, too close to be avoided. Three fast ground cars bearing the flags and insignia of Port Authority came sweeping up and then pushed a way through the crowd. A batch of Port police got out, and four Phalian officials of various sorts, and Arrikon.

The police began instantly to disperse the too-curious crowd. Arrikon pointed to Barron and DeWalt.

"Those are the two ring-leaders." He named them. "They took the girl away from me by force, and I demand her return."

All the time he was talking his eyes were on the ship, looking, thinking, gleaming with a hot spark of greedy inspiration. And Barron knew that he had not guessed wrong about Arrikon.

The officials came forward, flanked by the police.

"Are you Harley DeWalt and Samuel Barron?"

They admitted they were.

"A very serious charge has been laid against you," one of the officials said. He was a typical Pahlian, his palms worn as slippery-smooth as his conscience by the graft that had passed over them. Just now it was obvious that he and Arrikon had a working arrangement. He, too, looked up at the weirdly truncated ship, and his eyes, like Arrikon's glittered and gleamed.

"We understand you have aboard a citizen of Esha-Sirritt in the Pleiades, a woman named Laryl. We understand you're holding her by force. We also understand—" and here he nodded at the ruined ship—"that you constitute a threat to the safety and security of Pahlia, and that seems obvious. Therefore you will all be placed in custody pending further investigation."

Barron said, "We have a woman aboard all right, but I don't think it could be the same one this man is talking about." Barron smiled blandly at Arrikon. "He's made some mistake. I've certainly never seen him before. Wait, I'll bring the woman out and show you."

He turned swiftly and with DeWalt leaped inside the port before anybody thought to stop him. Lucich and Ybra were standing at the back of the lock chamber with Laryl, looking grim. Barron took the girl's hands.

"You heard all that?"

She nodded. "They're going to put us all in jail."

"Us," said Barron. "But not you. Arrikon has made some kind of a deal with the Pahlians. They're working together, and all their tongues are fairly hanging out. I don't think you're going to jail, and I don't think you're going to Esha. You'll go with Arrikon, and they'll use your power to the limit."

Tears came into Laryl's eyes again and she began to wail. "I don't want to go with him. I can't use the power that way. I'm afraid—"

"Oh, stop that and listen to me," Barron said impatiently, but the sniffling sobs continued.

"My ship," said DeWalt wrathfully. "And probably my neck in jail, too. I'll give her something to bawl about—"

A ROARING NOISE went overhead and Lucich darted to the well to look up. He came hopping back. "That's *Starlady* coming in—Viji's landing over on the west side of the field." And he added dismally, "A fat chance we have of ever getting to her now."

"Quit croaking and get that helix, fast," said Barron. "Yes, the one Laryl was using. Jump."

"Oh, now, listen," said DeWalt, "you're not going crazy, are you? This dame is dynamite when she has that gadget. Look what she did to my—"

"Have you got any better ideas?" demanded Barron. He turned to Laryl. He said, "There's only one way we can hold back that bunch out there, long enough for us to get to *Starlady*."

Laryl shook her head. "No, I couldn't do what you're thinking. I just couldn't. The power must never be used for gain or—"

"I know, for your own advantage," Barron interrupted. "But you've got to, this time."

Her trembling lower lip came out in a faintly mulish expression, "I couldn't. It's forbidden."

DeWalt swore lividly, but Barron paid him no attention. "Listen, it's to keep the power itself from being used by Arrikon and those others. Aren't you supposed to guard the power, to protect it?"

She looked at him, troubled and confused by that. Of a sudden, Barron felt an unexpected warm pity for her. She might not be too terribly bright, but she had got into all this by a very human desire to be something other than a Keeper, and she was very worried and lovely.

A peremptory voice called from outside. "Bring the girl out and give yourselves up!"

It decided Laryl. She looked at Barron and said in a whisper, "Am I to destroy them all—everything out there?"

"Good God, *no*," he said. "But do anything that will drive them back, keep them from following us until we get away in *Starlady*."

Lucich hurried in with the helix, holding it as though it were a reptile of a very venomous sort. Barron took it and handed it to Laryl.

She sat down on the floor of the lock, facing the outside, and again took the two wires in her hands. She shut her eyes and frowned. After a second she opened them again and shook her head.

"I'm so nervous," she said. "I can't think."

DeWalt swore, Barron crouched down beside her. He put his hand on her shoulder and said soothingly.

"Yes, you can. You can think, Laryl. Something to stop them. Something to hold them back."

Her eyes went shut again. "Something to hold. Something—"

She fell silent and the tip of her tongue crept out between her teeth.

From outside came a sharp questioning cry.

Laryl smiled. "Lovely," she whispered to herself. "Soft and pretty. Big. Big."

From outside, all at once, loud and spreading, the voice of panic.

Barron peered through the lock door. At first he wasn't sure what he was looking at. Around the far edges where the crowd had been pushed there was great activity, an outward surge of people scampering quickly away. Closer to *Vagabond*, where the police and the officials and Arrikon were, there was an area of shimmering uncertainty. It was something like a silvery gray fog, and something like pellucid water, and it enveloped Arrikon, the police and the officials. Their figures moved in it darkly, wildly, but the fog or water or whatever it was had substance too. Perhaps if you were inside it, it would seem more like a sliding gelatinous semi-solid. Its rising tide trapped their feet and hampered the movement of their legs, and it began to move slowly as though some wind was pushing it back away from *Vagabond* and toward the crowd, growing and billowing as it went, its spreading edges glittering prettily in the floodlights.

Barron could hear the men caught by that glittering, rising tide yelling loudly. The stuff was spreading fast now, faster than the crowd could run, rolling in shining waves toward other ships. Laryl was becoming intoxicated with her own power. Barron, a cold feeling at his spine, went back to her and shook her gently. "That's enough," he said. "That's fine."

She sighed and let the helix droop. "It felt so nice," she said. "I was enjoying that."

"Yes," said Barron. "But we have to go now. One of their cars is in the clear now—we can use that."

They went hurriedly out of the lock. The pearly tide had stopped rising and spreading. It looked very queer, gleaming in its arrested waves in the middle of the steel-and-concrete docks, with panicky people still fighting their way back out of it. Laryl was fascinated. Barron had almost to lift her into the car.

"That's the first time I've really created anything all on my own," she said. "Without any supervision, I mean. Usually it's a community effort—we Keepers all build together and then tear it all down."

"It's wonderful," Barron said tightly, and sent the car barreling away fast along the row of docks toward the landing field.

Starlady had touched down on the west side. Nobody tried to stop them and there was no pursuit at all yet from the panicky mess behind them. The car screeched to the side of *Starlady* as the lock opened.

Barron almost knocked Viji down getting in. "I'll explain later," he told him. "Right now we've got to move. See that everybody's snugged down. Take-off right now."

He rushed into the bridge with Lucich, hit the warning siren once and then slammed down the main jet control. He heaved a sigh of relief as the rockets fired and the tremendous surge of power pressed him down into the recoil-chair and pressed and pressed until he was blind and breathless with it. *Starlady* was up and away.

Space took her in. Wide dark cleanly space, with Pahlia's star a golden sunburst at her back and the Pleiades wrapped in burning mist ahead of her, indescribably beautiful and strange. Barron looked at them and loved them, every one of the Seven Sisters and their two thousand friends.

"They'll be after us," Lucich said gloomily. "That Arrikon ain't the kind to let a good thing go, and he's got the Pahlians to help, and that's bad. They're worse than wolves on the track of money."

"I know," Barron said. "But with any luck, any luck at all, we ought to be able to reach Esha before they catch up with us."

A voice behind him spoke, clearly and with a note of absolute resolve.

"We're not going to Esha."

He turned around.

"I've made up my mind," Laryl said. "I've done so wrong already that I might as well go the whole way. And I know now what I can do. I can do anything. Anything I want."

Her eyes shone with a bright blue light. She stood in the entrance to the bridge, her hair falling over her white shoulders and her filmy gown most enticingly torn by the violent activities of the past hours. Clutched against her magnificent bosom she held, with fierce pride and awareness of power, the lopsided helix.

She looked at Barron, and she smiled.

CHAPTER EIGHT

WHAT LARYL HAD DECIDED on, Laryl got. She held the helix in her pretty hands and said, "We'll go to Vega." And they went that way.

Barron tried to reason with her. "*Starlady* is a freighter. She's slow, and Vega is a very long way off. Arrikon and the Pahlians will have fast ships. We won't have a chance to outrun them."

"I stopped them before," she said. "I can stop them again."

Barron said, "It'll take more than a wave of whatever that stuff was, to stop spaceships. And this time they'll be on guard against that."

"I can stop them."

And that was that.

Red DeWalt tried force. The helix had been taken away from her once before by that method. But she had learned, too. He crept up behind her but she was watching, and before he could knock it out of her hands he was trapped as effectively as Arrikon had been, by the same strange and instantly created semi-solidity. He did not try it again. Neither did anyone else.

Starlady lumbered at her best matronly speed toward Vega. Barron kept a constant watch on radar and quarreled bitterly with DeWalt. "The next time," he said, "that a cute chick comes up to you and asks to be taken away from where she is, do me a favor? Tell her to go jump down the nearest well."

"Do me a favor," said DeWalt. "Will you? Just a little one. Shut up!"

Laryl lounged in the best cabin, which had once been Barron's hugging the helix and enjoying herself.

She had abandoned herself wholly to sin and the delights of power. "I'll never use it to hurt anyone," she said, "nor to make money, but after all the power is mine, isn't it? And why shouldn't I get something out of it for myself?"

And she dreamed dreams. Vega was the hub and center of the galaxy, rich, dazzling, full of excitement. Laryl saw herself, arrayed in a succession of magnificent costumes, dancing all night on crystal floors, being entertained by hosts of handsome men, moving like a bright star through a glitter of rather vague but delightful things. "I'll do all the things I used to imagine when I was back in our village on Esha," she said. "I'll see all the places and meet all the people. I'll really *live*, for the first time in my whole life. It'll be lots better than Pahlia."

She babbled happily on and on, and Barron, who was sure she could be the belle of the ball anywhere even without her helix, couldn't find it in his heart to blame her. The College had made a damned poor choice when they picked her for a life of dedicated seclusion. But if he could have got her pretty white neck between his hands, he would have wrung it all the same. Laryl might dance on tables all over Vega's eight worlds, but he didn't see what he would be doing, nor any of the other Earthmen of the Pleiades, with the ports shut in their faces and no place to go.

He tried appealing to her on that score, but she only said reasonably enough that after all they were big strong men and would have to look out for themselves.

"And after all," she said, "they didn't ask me if I wanted to be a Keeper."

Space stretched on ahead, and on all sides, and behind, sparsely populated in this sector with suns. Barron watched the ultrascopes, and inevitably he was rewarded by the sight of three unmistakable blips, moving together and at a steady rate of speed far exceeding that of *Starlady* on precisely the same course.

He showed them to the others and Dewalt said, "We can't outrun 'em, that's for sure. So?"

"So there's a cluster of wild stars about here," Barron said, working with the stereo chart and showing a related group of five suns almost at right angles to their present course. "Chart shows considerable nebulosity and dust concentration. If we run in there we might foul up their radar enough to dodge them."

Lucich said sourly that they might as well get shot running as sitting.

They changed course, sharply.

THE JARRING of the lateral thrust vortices—they were in overdrive—brought Laryl steaming out of her cabin.

"Why are we turning?" she demanded.

Barron explained. She wanted to be shown the blips on the ultrascope screen, which were now in the act of shifting course to match *Starlady*'s move, and were quite obviously overhauling her. Laryl made a gesture of superb contempt.

"Go on to Vega," she said. "I'll take care of them."

She faced *Starlady*'s stern and lifted the helix.

Barron said uneasily, "You're not in normal space now, you know. There isn't the same balance here between free particles and free energy and solid matter. Even the scientists don't understand what goes on in these ultra-speed warps. So take it easy—"

"Just go on to Vega," she said, and shut her eyes.

Barron began to sweat.

The three blips on the screen sped forward undisturbed.

Viji came running frantic from the drive-chamber aft. "She's heating. The whole assembly, the main coil housing, even the walls. She'll blow—"

He saw Laryl and what she was doing. His wizened face became even more ashen than before.

"It's her," he said. "What she's doing. This isn't normal space. The warp is damping all that energy output, and it's dissipating as heat. If you don't stop her, we'll burn up…"

Even the air in the bridge was hot now. Barron shouted, *"Laryl!"* But she was deep, deep in her supreme effort at concentration. The helix glowed red-hot, turning white at the tip.

Barron whispered, *"For God's sake."*

He launched himself at her in a flying tackle, from the side.

He was not at all clear about what happened after that. He thought at first that *Starlady* had blown up in his face. But after a while he realized that that couldn't be so because if you blew up in hyperspace there were not even whole atoms of you left, let alone whole pieces. He lifted his head slowly and looked around.

Ybra, Lucich, DeWalt and Viji were all huddled back against the farthest wall of the bridge. They were staring with four pairs of popping eyes out of four terrified faces. It was noticeably cooler. The helix, somewhat battered, lay under the ultrascope. Laryl was lying on her side, rubbing her uppermost hip and crying like a startled child.

"There, there," he said, and took her in his arms. "I didn't mean to hurt you, honey. Didn't you see what was happening? I told you this was a different kind of space. You weren't getting through. The ship was starting to burn up—"

Viji scuttled out and went back to his drive. The proximity-warning system set a whole battery of red lights flashing all over the bridge. Even in the warp it was possible to detect the slight fraction of additional warp added by the presence of massive bodies with massive magnetic fields. In other words, stars. They were close to the group, and it was time to cut the overdrive.

"Take her through, Red," he said to DeWalt, and DeWalt sat down in the pilot's seat.

"You hurt me," Laryl said.

She said it so much in the fashion of a child that he cradled her head on his shoulder and held it there. It felt nice. He put his other arm around her waist. That felt nice, too. "I'm sorry," he said into her tumbled hair. "But I couldn't let you go up in smoke, could I?"

"I don't believe you," she said with a sudden unreasoning fierceness that also was childlike. "You're just determined to take me back to Esha and you don't care how you do it."

She pounded on his face and chest with her hands, her cheeks red with rage.

For the life of him, Barron couldn't resist kissing her hard on the lips.

They tasted salty. Someone really ought to break her of that crying habit. She continued to fight him, and then of a sudden it happened.

DeWalt took the ship out of overdrive and into normal space.

The shock was always vertiginous and unpleasant. Barron lost track of what he was doing for a second or two, and that gave Laryl a chance for a convulsive movement. He grabbed wildly for her but by the time he caught her again she had got her hand on the helix.

"If you won't take me to Vega we won't go anywhere," she cried, and there was a wild lurching as something happened to *Starlady*. Barron hit Laryl hard on the side of the head. *Starlady* began to spiral, rolling over and over like an ungainly porpoise. There was a tremendous amount of noise. Barron clawed his way in a cold panic across the bridge to the pilot's chair. Red DeWalt was not in it now. Lucich was frozen to the co-pilot's seat, not doing anything, just hanging on. There was a planet where no planet should have been, ahead or right under them, whichever you wanted to call it. It belonged to a sun that burned like a big ugly furnace in a sooty cloud of dust. Barron grabbed for the controls.

The main tubes were dead. He thought probably Laryl had unmade them like she had unmade the forward part of *Vagabond*. He considered the possibility, for a fractional second, of trying to force her to re-make them, and decided against it. You could tear a thing down perfectly well without understanding it, but to build any part of an operating spaceship you had to understand it, and he did not want to depend on any main blast tubes that Laryl put together out of her own head. Anyway, she was still dazed from the clout he had given her.

THERE WERE CRIES of pain, dismay and protest from various parts of the ship. He ignored them. The planet was falling up at him at a frightening rate of speed. He saw it as a dirty-green ball, like verdigrised copper, fairly springing at him out of the dark-glowing stellar dust. He hit the lateral jets, talking to *Starlady* with incoherent curses and pleas to stop her damned corkscrewing. She obeyed him finally, with a heavy rattling of her plates, and went wallowing down into the copper-colored sky on an even keel.

She was still going too fast. He did everything he could to slow her down. He did things he didn't know you could do with a ship, using nose and steering jets for purposes that had never been intended in their engineering. And he did slow her down, enough so that when she came booming down out of a thick overcast and through a driving rain to hit the close-packed mat of a forest, she crumpled the trees under her quite gently and came to rest at the end of a long torn swath, lying prone with every joint in her ancient frame sprung wide and her belly ripped open and spilling cargo into the mud. But she was still a ship, and not a smoking pile of junk.

After a while the people in her began to stir, all except one of the mechanics, who was hurt, and Laryl, who had been knocked totally unconscious. DeWalt was swearing viciously over a broken wrist. Ybra looked at Barron and grinned and said, "You were right. I should have stayed home." Blood was running from his nose as water runs from a tap, and there was a blackening welt running right across his face under the eyes. He was only grinning to keep himself from crying.

Barron pried himself out of the chair. He felt as though his every joint was sprung like *Starlady*'s, and every bone shattered, but since he was able to get up and move that was obviously impossible. He helped Lucich up, Lucich was groggy, but he did not seem injured. The hurt mechanic had a dislocated shoulder, but the other mechanic and the electronics man and Viji were all right.

Viji glared at the crumpled form of the unconscious girl and said, "You know what happened, Sam. All of a sudden no tubes, no jets. Like that, gone. She killed a good ship."

"Two good ships," said DeWalt. "And damn near got us, too. We ought to—"

"Yes," Barron said, "we ought to, but we won't. And besides we may need her and her gifted so-called mind. Where's that helix?"

DeWalt cried out to heaven. "Look what happened the last time you gave it to her. Why don't you just shoot us all now and be done with it?"

Barron heaved the girl's inert body into his arms and said, "If we can fight off Arrikon and the Pahlians without her I won't dream of it. But find that helix. You," he said to the uninjured mechanic, "break out the first-aid box and some rations and fill all the thermo-bottles with water. Help him, Ybra. Hop to it. Viji, break out the ship's armament."

Imposing words, which when translated meant three EP handguns and two rifles, with not unlimited ammunition.

He carried Laryl out of the bridge and along the buckled central well. The lock was burst open. A rank smell of wetness and greenness and mud came in, with the sound of rain. There had not been any time to test the atmosphere, nor any use of testing it, since whatever it was they were stuck with it. So far it did not seem poisonous in any way, and the forest was a good indication. He eased Laryl down into the mud, jumped down himself, and helped DeWalt down after him.

There was a roaring, ripping thunder across the sky. Barron looked up. The clouds were riven apart, once, twice, three times in close succession, showing the metallic bellies of three ships.

Arrikon and the Pahlians, looking for a place to land.

CHAPTER NINE

IT WAS, BARRON THOUGHT, one hell of a world.

The rain had stopped. The sun shone through broken clouds, a huge sulfurous fiery thing that was only prevented from setting the whole planet ablaze by the heavy concentration of dust that occluded it, tempering its heat. The wet ground steamed. The forest, or jungle, steamed too. It was one of those vile-looking places, bloated and gorged with heat, water, and good rotting humus so that even the trees were fat.

Barron led the way through it, his lungs laboring against the semi-liquid air. The others straggled and struggled behind. The men had had to take turns carrying Laryl, all except DeWalt and the mechanic with the hurt shoulder. It was Viji's turn now, and Barron kept looking around to make sure he had not quietly dropped her into a convenient pool. She was still out cold, and he found himself strangely distressed about it. In spite of all she had done he could not bear the thought of her being really hurt.

Floundering through green algae up to his thighs, he wondered if he was in love with her.

Fat lot of good it would do him if he was.

"How much farther?" asked DeWalt. Viji had splinted his wrist and given him a shot but he was almost as pale as the injured mechanic.

Barron said, "Just a little way."

"Wouldn't it have been better," asked Ybra diffidently, "to scatter out and hide in the jungle? I don't see how they could ever find us in this mess."

Barron shook his head. "They'd beat the bushes, till they did. They've got all the men and all the time they need. We don't have either. They'll blow what's left of *Starlady* first thing, which means we'll have no supplies to fall back on. Besides, that's what they'd expect us to do. The last thing they'll be looking for is for us to attack them."

He did not state the real reason, which was that he was sick and tired of running.

The trees and the rank creepers thinned a bit over a rib of rock. A jagged tumbled cliff of black basalt lifted up in a long line capped with a spire that looked from this angle as though it had speared the lopsided sun.

"There," said Barron.

They scrambled up and in among the slabs of rock. Barron had found the cliff less than a mile from *Starlady*, and when he had climbed it he had been able to see how the jungle gave way to a rising plain dotted but not drowned with trees. He had seen the three ships of the Pahlians and the man from Altair standing on the plain, and he had decided that the cliff would be as good a place to make a stand as any. Arrikon and the Pahlians would almost have to come this way—it was both the straightest and the easiest path to the wrecked *Starlady*.

They disposed themselves along the face of the cliff wherever the rock offered shelter, keeping a lookout for the sort of creature that inhabits such places. They killed several of a particular nastiness, including a pair of snake-like things about ten feet long and no thicker than wire. Clouds lay in weird heavy layers above the horizon, colored strangely with tints of green and ochre and sooty gray on the lower tiers. Higher up, the sun bled red all over the sky. It was, Barron thought again, one hell of a world.

They had shared out the guns and ammunition. Barron had one of the rifles, Lucich the other. Ybra, Viji and the uninjured mechanic, whose name was Srann, had the handguns. DeWalt and the hurt mechanic they put in a safe niche of the rock with Laryl, both of them too sick to object.

Laryl was still unconscious. An ugly purple goose egg disfigured her lovely forehead. Barron felt her pulse worriedly. It seemed strong, and her breathing was regular. He put the softest pack under her head for a pillow. DeWalt watched him sardonically but did not say anything.

Lucich, who had been carrying the thing hitched to his own pack, handed the helix to DeWalt.

Barron took up a post near the niche. He could see Ybra's white crest, muddy and draggled now, a little below him and to his right. If he lifted his gaze he could see the ships out on the plain. It was dreadfully hot. Sweat gathered and dripped off the end of his nose.

HE SAW MEN MOVING in the sparse jungle along the line of the cliff, coming closer.

"Shoot for the leaders," Barron said quietly. "And don't waste your shots."

He, wiped his sodden sleeve across his face and laid his rifle along the basalt slab.

He looked for Arrikon.

He saw him, distinguished by his height and leanness from the shorter Pahlians. He waited with stony patience for him to come within range, and even while he did so he realized the futility of it. Arrikon might die. The Pahlians might die. But if Laryl survived, other Arrikons and other Pahlians would spring up, as ruthless and greedy as they, lusting not after her beauty but after the incredible power of her mind that could make any man who controlled it an emperor above emperors, a demi-god to stride the galaxy. Now that her secret was out, she would never be safe again, unless he could get her back to the cloisters of The College on Esha, where she would have a whole world and others of her kind to protect her.

He aimed for the center of Arrikon's chest. With explosive pellets there was no need for precision. And as he did so he saw Arrikon look up suddenly at the cliff—perhaps some slight sound or movement had betrayed the ambush, or perhaps it was only that Arrikon had realized the possibilities offered by that somber pile of rock. Whichever it was, he made a long leap that took him behind a tree and sent Barron's missile whizzing past him to burst harmlessly against another trunk.

The ambush was not a total loss. They shot two of the Pahlian leaders and three of the thirty or so men who were with them, before they could find an adequate cover.

The return barrage popped and banged, but all Barron's men had to do was stay out of sight in their holes.

So far, so good.

Silence.

The metallic voice of a portable loudspeaker boomed out from among the trees.

"You're hopelessly outnumbered," it said, in what was unmistakably Arrikon's voice. "And we can hold you there until you starve or die of thirst."

Barron shouted back, his voice echoing dully from the cliff. "Sure," he said. "But it'll take a long time. How many of you will be left by then?"

He snapped a shot toward the sound of the loudspeaker, stirring up some hasty movement in the brush.

"Listen," said Arrikon. "We don't want you or your friends. We only want the girl. Send her down and we'll let you go. We'll even give you a lifeboat."

"No," said Barron. "I'm taking her back to Esha."

Arrikon laughed. "Let's not be silly, Barron. Nobody's taking her back to Esha. I'll make a deal." He corrected himself. "*We'll* make a deal, my partners and I."

"I'm listening."

"We split four ways. You, me, and my two partners. Make your own arrangements with your friends. What that girl has ought to be more than enough for all of us. Well?"

Barron was suddenly delivered of a lunatic inspiration.

"That's fine," he shouted. "I'd love to. But there's one little hitch." He took a deep breath and yelled it out. "The girl's dead. It's only her body I'm taking to Esha."

He turned and ducked into the niche. DeWalt was staring at him as though he had gone crazy. Barron muttered, "She looks limp enough to be dead, and Lord knows she's heavy enough. Maybe it'll fool them."

He picked Laryl up, letting her arms and her head with its banner of red hair hang down. He carried her out where everyone could see.

"She was hurt in the crash, and died," he shouted. "So now we have nothing to fight about, have we?"

Silence.

Laryl hung heavy in his arms and the wind blew her hair and fluttered her garment.

"Leave us that lifeboat," Barron shouted, "and we'll take her body back to Esha."

Silence again.

Ybra looked up, wide-eyed and hopeful. Barron held his breath.

It might, just possibly, have worked. But Barron never knew, because that was when the first glimmer of consciousness returned to Laryl. She waved her arms and moaned, twisting around in Barron's grasp, and that was the end of that.

HE FELL BACK with her into the niche. A howl of anger went up from the men below, and almost immediately they rushed the cliff. Missiles began to burst like exploding hail.

Laryl held her head between her hands and whispered, "What's happened?"

"You've got us all killed with your damned stubbornness, that's what," said Barron furiously. "You wrecked the ship and now they're going to finish us off and take you, and I hope you're happy." He was so glad she was all right that he could have strangled her. He picked up his rifle and went out on the cliff again.

There were men below clambering among the rocks. There were other men among the trees firing a steady barrage of missiles to keep the defenders down while the climbers got within striking distance. Barron was too angry and hopeless now to worry. He fired down the cliff, exposing himself with moderate recklessness in the hope of getting one more shot at Arrikon. But he didn't see him, and one by one the guns on the cliff stopped firing as his men ran out of ammunition.

And then, suddenly, it began to rain rocks out of the sky.

The rocks fell straight downward out of the nothingness above, crashing and banging among the trees, tearing off branches, and everything else came to a stupefied standstill for a moment. Then there was a rising chorus of shouts, and men began to run out from among the trees and scatter wildly. And the rocks came down, crash, crash, crash.

Somebody screamed, "Look at the ships!"

It was raining rocks there, too. Big ones, house-sized rocks, battering the metal hulls.

Barron turned and peered into the niche. Laryl held the helix, and her face had a brooding look.

"By God," cried DeWalt, his face aflame. "She's doing it—she's done it—"

Down at the foot of the cliff Arrikon gathered a small party of men and came swarming up. The man from Altair had not panicked. The sky could fall but he was not to be swerved. He dodged the falling stones and kept climbing even when the men around him were swept away.

He glimpsed Barron and shot fast, and the exploding missile seared the rock beside Barron, scorching his face. Half-blinded, he shot back by instinct. When he could see, Arrikon lay still.

That seemed to do it. The last men below took flight, carrying their wounded and running like rabbits toward the doubtful protection of their battered ships. Barron went into the niche.

"That's enough," he said to Laryl. "Stop it."

She appeared not to hear him.

He raised his voice one notch, not very loud, and said, "Laryl."

Her eyes opened and she glanced at him.

"I said, that's enough."

Her chin quivered. "All right, Sam," she said, and dropped the helix. "I—I didn't really mean what I said on the ship. And I'm sorry I wrecked it—I don't really hate you. And my head hurts, and I'm miserable, and—"

He took her in his arms, and she started that damned crying again.

One by one, out on the plain, the ships took off. For now, Barron knew, they were safe. With all or most of their leaders gone the men would be too disorganized to make any more attempts in the face of Laryl's power.

Barron leaned over and picked up the helix. "They never had a chance to blow the wreck," he said, "so we can hold out in here fine for a while. We'll get that radio fixed and then we'll soon be picked up."

Laryl's eyes were pleading. "And then—"

He could not meet her eyes. "Laryl, you wouldn't be safe anywhere in the galaxy now, except on Esha. I hate it too. But—you must go back."

CHAPTER TEN

MANY DAYS LATER, Barron paced up and down the green terrace outside The College on Esha. He kept looking at the blank white front of the building, and when he couldn't see anything he paced the harder, uneasy and increasingly upset.

They had told him firmly to wait.

It had been a tough time for Barron emotionally since the day of that last fight on the cliff. Viji and the mechanic had managed to patch up *Starlady*'s radio, and then they had not had to wait too long for rescue. The rescue ship had passed them on to one of the Pleiad traders, Old Man Kirk, and Kirk had brought them to Esha—after lengthy talks by radio with the heads of The College, who had promised on solemn oaths that no harm of any sort would come to Laryl if he brought her in.

The Pleiades were open again. The traders could trade, and everything was going to be just as it had been before. Even the loss of *Vagabond* and *Starlady* and their cargoes were to be indemnified by The College, in view of the services of DeWalt and Barron in bringing Laryl back. They were satisfied now that DeWalt had been a more or less innocent victim of Laryl's wiles, with no intent to use her power.

So he had given Laryl back to the safety of The College, and they had told him to wait. And everything was going to be just as it had been before, except that now he was in love with Laryl, and so nothing would ever be the same again. And he didn't know what he was waiting for.

What were they doing to her in there?

He paced and sweated and fretted and finally he could not stand it any longer. He went and beat with the heavy knocker on the great bronze door.

It opened and two priests came running through it, making motions for him to stop.

"It is almost finished," one of them said. "Hush, or you'll disturb them."

"What's almost finished?" Barron demanded. He reached out savagely. "What are they doing to her? You promised—"

"Please," said the priest. "She's perfectly safe. But it is now obvious that we made a serious mistake when we chose her as a Keeper, in spite of her remarkable power. In every other part of her she is totally unsuited to the office. So we are going to release her. But first she must be made safe. Her power of psycho-creation must be taken from her."

"Taken from her?" asked Barron, more than ever alarmed. "How could you do that, when it's in her mind—"

The priest smiled thinly. "The power of the other six Keepers can do even that. It is a necessary safeguard. They are rearranging the synaptic pattern of her brain, so that when she wakes again she will no longer have the power she had, nor the memory of how it felt to use it, nor the wish to have it ever again. So she will not be a menace either to herself or others. Now will you be patient?"

Barron waited, not patiently but with a great hope dawning in him, with a whole new future suddenly presented to him.

And after a while she came, running down the broad green terrace from The College, into his arms.

Barron said, *"Must* you always cry?" And then he said, "Go ahead and cry, Laryl. I can always get used to that."

THE END

If you've enjoyed this book, you will not want to miss these terrific titles...

ARMCHAIR SCI-FI & HORROR DOUBLE NOVELS, $12.95 each

D-1 **THE GALAXY RAIDERS** by William P. McGivern
SPACE STATION #1 by Frank Belknap Long

D-2 **THE PROGRAMMED PEOPLE** by Jack Sharkey
SLAVES OF THE CRYSTAL BRAIN by William Carter Sawtelle

D-3 **YOU'RE ALL ALONE** by Fritz Leiber
THE LIQUID MAN by Bernard C. Gilford

D-4 **CITADEL OF THE STAR LORDS** by Edmond Hamilton
VOYAGE TO ETERNITY by Milton Lesser

D-5 **IRON MEN OF VENUS** by Don Wilcox
THE MAN WITH ABSOLUTE MOTION by Noel Loomis

D-6 **WHO SOWS THE WIND...** by Rog Phillips
THE PUZZLE PLANET by Robert A. W. Lowndes

D-7 **PLANET OF DREAD** by Murray Leinster
TWICE UPON A TIME by Charles L. Fontenay

D-8 **THE TERROR OUT OF SPACE** by Dwight V. Swain
QUEST OF THE GOLDEN APE by Paul W. Fairman & Milton Lesser

D-9 **SECRET OF MARRACOTT DEEP** by Henry Slesar
PAWN OF THE BLACK FLEET by Mark Clifton.

D-10 **BEYOND THE RINGS OF SATURN** by Robert Moore Williams
A MAN OBSESSED by Alan E. Nourse

ARMCHAIR SCIENCE FICTION CLASSICS, $12.95 each

C-1 **THE GREEN MAN**
by Harold M. Sherman

C-2 **A TRACE OF MEMORY**
By Keith Laumer

C-3 **INTO PLUTONIAN DEPTHS**
by Stanton A. Coblentz

ARMCHAIR MASTERS OF SCIENCE FICTION SERIES, $16.95 each

M-1 **MASTERS OF SCIENCE FICTION, Vol. One**
Bryce Walton—"Dark of the Moon" and other tales

M-2 **MASTERS OF SCIENCE FICTION, Vol. Two**
Jerome Bixby—"One Way Street" and other tales

If you've enjoyed this book, you will not want to miss these terrific titles…

ARMCHAIR SCI-FI & HORROR DOUBLE NOVELS, $12.95 each

D-11   **PERIL OF THE STARMEN** by Kris Neville
THE STRANGE INVASION by Murray Leinster

D-12   **THE STAR LORD** by Boyd Ellanby
CAPTIVES OF THE FLAME by Samuel R. Delany

D-13   **MEN OF THE MORNING STAR** by Edmond Hamilton
PLANET FOR PLUNDER by Hal Clement and Sam Merwin, Jr.

D-14   **ICE CITY OF THE GORGON** by Chester S. Geier and Richard Shaver
WHEN THE WORLD TOTTERED by Lester del Rey

D-15   **WORLDS WITHOUT END** by Clifford D. Simak
THE LAVENDER VINE OF DEATH by Don Wilcox

D-16   **SHADOW ON THE MOON** by Joe Gibson
ARMAGEDDON EARTH by Geoff St. Reynard

D-17   **THE GIRL WHO LOVED DEATH** by Paul W. Fairman
SLAVE PLANET by Laurence M. Janifer

D-18   **SECOND CHANCE** by J. F. Bone
MISSION TO A DISTANT STAR by Frank Belknap Long

D-19   **THE SYNDIC** by C. M. Kornbluth
FLIGHT TO FOREVER by Poul Anderson

D-20   **SOMEWHERE I'LL FIND YOU** by Milton Lesser
THE TIME ARMADA by Fox B. Holden

ARMCHAIR SCIENCE FICTION CLASSICS, $12.95 each

C-4   **CORPUS EARTHLING**
by Louis Charbonneau

C-5   **THE TIME DISSOLVER**
by Jerry Sohl

C-6   **WEST OF THE SUN**
by Edgar Pangborn

ARMCHAIR SCI-FI & HORROR GEMS SERIES, $12.95 each

G-1   **SCIENCE FICTION GEMS, Vol. One**
Isaac Asimov and others

G-2   **HORROR GEMS, Vol. One**
Carl Jacobi and others

If you've enjoyed this book, you will not want to miss these terrific titles…

ARMCHAIR SCI-FI & HORROR DOUBLE NOVELS, $12.95 each

D-91 **THE TIME TRAP** by Henry Kuttner
THE LUNAR LICHEN by Hal Clement

D-92 **SARGASSO OF LOST STARSHIPS** by Poul Anderson
THE ICE QUEEN by Don Wilcox

D-93 **THE PRINCE OF SPACE** by Jack Williamson
POWER by Harl Vincent

D-94 **PLANET OF NO RETURN** by Howard Browne
THE ANNIHILATOR COMES by Ed Earl Repp

D-95 **THE SINISTER INVASION** by Edmond Hamilton
OPERATION TERROR by Murray Leinster

D-96 **TRANSIENT** by Ward Moore
THE WORLD-MOVER by George O. Smith

D-97 **FORTY DAYS HAS SEPTEMBER** by Milton Lesser
THE DEVIL'S PLANET by David Wright O'Brien

D-98 **THE CYBERENE** by Rog Phillips
BADGE OF INFAMY by Lester del Rey

D-99 **THE JUSTICE OF MARTIN BRAND** by Raymond A. Palmer
BRING BACK MY BRAIN by Dwight V. Swain

D-100 **WIDE-OPEN PLANET** by L. Sprague de Camp
AND THEN THE TOWN TOOK OFF by Richard Wilson

ARMCHAIR SCIENCE FICTION CLASSICS, $12.95 each

C-31 **THE GOLDEN GUARDSMEN**
by S. J. Byrne

C-32 **ONE AGAINST THE MOON**
by Donald A. Wollheim

C-33 **HIDDEN CITY**
by Chester S. Geier

ARMCHAIR SCI-FI & HORROR GEMS SERIES, $12.95 each

G-9 **SCIENCE FICTION GEMS, Vol. Five**
Clifford D. Simak and others

G-10 **HORROR GEMS, Vol. Five**
E. Hoffman Price and others